SpaceTime 2047
By Peggy Luczak Grillot

Harlan Imprints, LLC
Columbia, South Carolina

SpaceTime 2047
April 2019
Print Edition

This is a work of fiction. Any similarity to actual persons, living or dead, companies, events, or locales is entirely coincidental. The book and its characters, places and incidents are products of the author's imagination or used fictitiously.

**Publisher's Cataloging-In-Publication Data**
(Prepared by The Donohue Group, Inc.)

Names: Grillot, Peggy Luczak, author.
Title: SpaceTime 2047 / by Peggy Luczak Grillot.
Other Titles: Space time 2047
Description: Columbia, South Carolina : Harlan Imprints, LLC, 2019.
Identifiers: ISBN 9781948214063 | ISBN 9781948214056 (ebook)
Subjects: LCSH: Nursing home patients--Fiction. | Kidnapping--Fiction. |
    Criminal investigation--Fiction. | Space ships--Fiction.
Classification: LCC PS3607.R5548 S63 2019 (print) | LCC PS3607.R5548
    (ebook) | DDC 813/.6--dc23

To Gregory Steven Luczak,
may your star shine brightly
in the night sky.

This book is dedicated to Harlan Thomas Grillot, my soulmate, and to our children Logan and Wade, their spouses Dennis and Sarah, and to our grandchildren Aidan, Peyton, Skylar, Pyper, Wayland, Wyatt and Sawyer. May the thrill of a good story always be part of your lives.

To my dearest friends Marge, Dolly, Loreen, Vicki, Lynda, Colette, Phyllis, Burt, Beth, Marie, Paul and Ceni, thank you for being my sounding boards.

For the sisters and teachers at Divine Infant Elementary School and Immaculate Heart of Mary High School in Westchester, Illinois, thank you for the great education and love of the English language you instilled.

To Harry and Agnes Luczak, the best storytellers of all, thank you for being my parents. And to my brothers Greg and Bill, their wives Mary and Judy, and my nieces and nephews Katie, Matt, Taylor and Alex, thank you for being my support.

*Peggy*

# Chapter 1 – Westchester Community Care Center

I was in my 90s and so was my husband when they came for us. He had been living on life support and via Simon, his robot, in the community care home we shared. Our children kept asking me to pull the plug, but I was adamant something was going to change. The children were just as adamant I was the one who was going to change. They were in the process of declaring me incompetent so they could make that decision for me. Until then, I kept watch. I maintained a vigil by the side of his bed. I was his caregiver.

There were others here too, with walkers, wheelchairs, prosthetic limbs, falling bosoms, poor eyesight, dentures. Hair grew in all the wrong places. Some women had mustaches that rivaled the men's, bristly like kiwi. All had dreams of being young again. All we seemed to talk about at meal times were the good old days.

They, the ones who wanted us, posed as caretakers, nurses' aides, floor washers, dining room help. They made friends with us. They encouraged us to talk about the good old days. They listened when we talked to them; and they eavesdropped when we didn't.

They spent a lot of time helping my husband Thomas. He rarely spoke. His eyes were often closed, as if in deep contemplation. His robot Simon watched over him. Simon did not like the new staff, the ones who paid too much attention to us. He'd bristle and push them away, telling them to leave Thomas alone, that he was his ward and no one else's.

I didn't know what to make of it. I had long thought there would be a change, something new in the medical field, to bring my Thomas back to me, which is why I held on so long keeping him on life support.

There was a small article in the local news about inhabitants vanishing from another local community care center in the state. That article made three by my count but Simon said it was actually eleven.

"How is that possible?" I asked Simon. "I haven't seen that many articles."

"Remember I am attached to the world web. I have access to everything," Simon said matter-of-factly, with no emotion.

I turned my head quizzically, trying to make sense of what Simon had just told me.

A few nights later, while I pretended to be asleep with Thomas next to me in his own twin bed and Simon in his recharging station, one of the caretakers came in with another staff member. It was too late for a social call, so I peeked through the slits of my eyelids. They stood over Thomas, one on each side of his bed. The caretaker in pink scrubs rubbed her hand over his nipples and gauged his response, which was immediate. They smiled at each other. "This one," the one in pink scrubs said.

I thought they might stop over at my bed, but they just slipped out the door as quietly as they had come in. It took me a long while to fall asleep.

The next morning, I asked some of the other ladies at breakfast if they had any visitors. Ruth smiled and said, "Why yes! How did you know Herman came to see me?"

I blushed. I had no idea Ruth was seeing Herman. I turned to Lillian, "What about you?'

Before Lillian could respond, Ginny, the staffer who had been in my room last night smiled and asked, "And just WHAT about you?" But her smile did not reach her eyes and she kept watching me.

Lillian blustered and said she had crept out to watch an old movie in Eddie's room. We all cackled at that response, and I laughed louder than the others just to make a good show of it. Lillian asked me if I had any visitors. I hadn't expected that question but moved quickly to recover.

"Why no, Lillian. Thomas and I turned in early and we slept like babes, or at least I did," I smiled. The dining room staffer cleared our dishes with her robotic smile in place.

Lillian said, "Why Margaret, your hand is shaking."

I tried to hold my coffee cup still as I took a sip. "I must have had too much regular coffee yesterday," I murmured. And even though Ginny was at another table, clearing dishes, I swear she heard me.

Every time I tried to talk to another resident at the nursing home, Ginny seemed to be there. She'd adjust the blinds remotely in the great room. Then she'd be watering the greenery. Next time she was wiping down the computers. I finally gave up and headed toward my room. I was still in the hallway when my great grandson caught up and walked alongside me.

"Hello Great Nana," Aidan said to me. He just turned 18 and would be heading off to college in the fall.

I paused long enough so Aidan and I could hug. "Let's go see Great Papa," I suggested. We went into our little room.

Simon looked up and said, "Hello Master Aidan. Hello Margaret. Thomas just finished getting dressed."

Thomas was dressed smartly in a red and black flannel shirt, buttoned nearly to the neck. He had on pull-up jeans, something he would have hated if he had been able to talk. He was sitting up in a chair, with his eyes open, an unusual sight.

I maneuvered over to him and gave him a little peck on his cheek, saying, "Good morning, Thomas. Your favorite great grandson Aidan is here to see you."

As if on cue, Aidan piped up, "Good morning Great Papa," walked over and gave Great Papa a shoulder hug.

Great Papa had no reaction, but Simon said, "He knows you are here. He just can't express it." Simon put a little blanket on Thomas' legs. "Shall we go for a walk?" Pretending to hear a 'yes,' Simon positioned himself next to Thomas, flipped open a panel on his own robotic arm, and began to control Thomas' chair through a small joystick. Simon and Thomas headed toward the outside door, which was right past the nurses' station.

"Let's go with them," I suggested to Aidan. "I could use some fresh air myself." I grabbed my sweater and tablet. Aidan turned his head a bit, as if to ask 'why?' I shook my head, folding the tablet into my sweater pocket.

And it was a good thing too, because Ginny was right across from our door, watering the fern in the hallway. She didn't look up, but I knew she was listening.

"We're going outside for a quick stroll," I said to no one in particular. It may have been my imagination, but Ginny's shoulders seemed to sag a bit.

When we exited the building, I could see Ginny back at the nurse's station, looking out the front door. I waved brightly. I couldn't wait to tell my great grandson all that had been happening.

"Aidan, did you know residents are going missing from care centers?" I asked as we sat down on a green park bench near a little waterway.

"Really?" Aidan responded. "This sounds like one of your famous mysteries." He was referring to the fact that I had made my living as a writer. Of course, a little murder always helped to sell books.

"No, I'm serious." I unfolded my tablet to search for the news story I had been reading about the latest disappearance and I handed my tablet to Aidan.

After reading the story, Aidan shrugged his shoulders. "So maybe they all went off on a trip?"

"Master Aidan," Simon responded, "that article makes 11 centers where some of the residents disappeared."

"Eleven? Well, that does seem a bit unusual. So, do you have a theory, Great Nana?"

"Well, you know I do. I haven't worked it all out in my head yet, but I think they are being abducted by aliens."

Aidan, who had been sitting comfortably next to me, stood up. "Abducted by aliens?" he said so loudly I was sure Ginny inside could hear him.

"Ssssh. Sit down. I don't want the staff to hear you."

"Great Nana, are you working on another book and not telling me? 'Cause if that's the case, this is definitely going to be a bestseller."

I shook my head no. "I wish that were the case. Last night when we were sleeping, two of the staff came into our room. I pretended to be asleep. They stood over Thomas's bed and said, 'This one.' I think they're going to try to take Thomas. Of course, I won't let that happen. I will demand to go with them."

Aidan's eyes were as big as saucers. "What? You are going to let them kidnap you and Great Papa? I won't let that happen. I'll tell Momma."

"I'm afraid that won't do any good. Your momma would tell my daughter. And she and her husband are already trying to declare me incompetent so they can unplug Thomas. They think I'm batty."

Aidan snorted. "You're the most with-it person I know. That's a load of crap."

"I know, honey. I know. Don't be mad at your grandmother. She's only doing what she thinks best. I'm only telling you this so if Great Papa and I disappear, you know what happened."

"What about me?" Simon asks. "I can't leave Master Thomas."

I hadn't realized Simon was listening. "I haven't figured out how to take you along. The news article says they leave everything behind, phones, tablets, robots. Basically, they disappear with just the clothes they are wearing."

Aidan looked visibly shaken.

I tried to make light of it. "I've decided to start sleeping in my best outfits just in case they take me at night. I don't want to go in my pajamas. I don't know how long I'd have to wear them before they gave me something new."

Aidan smiled but he was still bothered. He was mulling over something in his head. "How am I going to talk to you if you are on an alien spaceship?"

"Unless you have some type of device that allows me to talk over space, I don't see how.'

He jumped up off the bench, running his hands over the back of his head. "But I do. I just bought a SpaceTime device." Aidan went on to explain how his girlfriend was doing an interspace internship on the moon. "Look, I'll give you the one I just bought. I'll just get another." He went to his red electric truck and grabbed a package off the passenger seat.

"Here, Great Nana. Now you can contact me if you're in space," Aidan said as he handed the device to me. Sitting down next to me, Aidan showed me a few features and how to work it.

Out of the corner of my eye, I could see Ginny heading toward us, shaking her head, so I hurriedly put the device into my sweater pocket.

"Master Thomas, isn't it about time you came inside? You're shivering," Ginny clucked, looking at us with her angry eyebrows and soulless shark eyes.

Simon picked up on her tone and seemed to cluck a bit himself. "Master Thomas, I did not notice you getting chilled. My oversight. We must head back where we can get you warmed up."

When I looked into Thomas' staring blue eyes, I saw real fear. He wasn't cold. He was scared. When he saw I recognized his fear, he shut his eyes, as if he could blot out what was going to happen.

Ginny started walking back briskly with Simon and Thomas in tow. She turned to look at me with raised eyebrows and a cocked head, as if to say, "Coming?" I answered even though the question was never asked. "I'll be in. I just want to say goodbye to my great grandson."

Aidan waited until they were at the door. I had my back to them and mouthed, "Are they inside?"

Aidan answered quietly, "No, not yet."

I put my fingers to my lips so he wouldn't say anymore until they were inside.

"What in tarnation was that all about?" Aidan asked angrily. "If that's how staff treats y'all, they should be reported."

"She's one of the two who came into our room. I think I might need Simon's help to come home from wherever they are taking us. How can I bring him with?"

"I can't believe you are just going to go with them! Can't we tell somebody so we can stop them?" Aidan asked.

"Sit down, hinny," I always used the word 'hinny' when I wanted my way and Aidan knew it. I sat back down on the bench and patted the seat next to me. I kept Thomas alive all these years for a reason. I think the aliens can help him since it seems obvious that they want something from him. So 'yes' if they are taking Thomas, I am going with him. Now you've given me the SpaceTime device so we can keep in touch and I can tell you what's going on. It might be that this is bigger than the local authorities. Then you'll have to be prepared to take it to the next level. But I would like to take Simon. From what I've read, though, none of the abductees have taken their personal robots, so how can I do that?"

Aidan thought about it for a moment and then said, "Well, you wouldn't have to take Simon himself, you could just take the important parts or rather part of him. You just need to take his intelligence chip."

"Okay. I actually know where that is. But how can I conceal it so they won't find it or the SpaceTime device either for that matter?" I asked.

Aidan said, "That's easy. Can I see the device again?" I handed it to him and he opened the back of it. "I'm pretty sure there's enough room to store a chip in here. Do you have a 3D printer onsite?"

He explained how I should make a wax image of Simon's intelligence chip and then insert the wax one into Simon to make a backup. Once that was done, I would just store the wax chip in the Space Time device. Aidan said the Space Time device has a game interface, so if they question me, I could just say it's a therapeutic game I play with Thomas.

Aidan stood up and turned just in time to see Ginny heading in our direction. "What does she want now?" he asked angrily.

I said, "Ssssh." I continued louder, "Oh Aidan, I so enjoyed your visit I lost track of time. I must be heading back to check on Thomas." I gave him a big long hug. Aidan hung onto me a bit longer and then said, "Let me take a picture of us." With our backs to the menacing Ginny who was stomping toward us, Aidan held his camera up and said, "Photo." He took a few and then I pecked him on the cheek, whispering, "I'll be in touch."

Ginny had stopped walking toward us once she saw us saying our goodbyes. Aidan had tears in his eyes. "Promise me you'll call," he said with a heavy heart.

"Of course, my dear. Don't be silly. I'll call you," I said loudly so Ginny could hear.

Once inside, I checked on Thomas. He was resting comfortably and Simon was doing a crossword puzzle, actually puzzles because he was so fast. I went back to sit in the lounge area, waiting for Ginny to take a lunch break. When I saw her leave, I headed back into our room to remove Simon's intelligence chip. Entering the media room, I put the chip on the 3D printer. I had to do it a few times before I figured out the correct procedure. Just as I finished, Ginny popped her head into the room. "Miss Margaret, the ladies are looking for you to play dominos." Her eyes traveled from the 3D printer to the chip in my hand and back. I made a big show about wadding up the wax and throwing it in the trash can right by Ginny. "Darn fool thing doesn't work a lick." I walked right past Ginny and headed to the card room. I stopped in long enough to let the ladies know I'd be right back after I checked on Thomas. I deftly slipped the wax intelligence chip back into Simon and tucked the real one in my bra. Simon didn't miss a beat. He started on the crossword puzzle where he left off.

I sat down at the card table with a loud sigh. "Margaret, are you all right? You look a little out of breath?" Ruth asked.

"Oh, I'm fine. Just getting a little old, I guess. But I guess you're not feeling so old Ruth, if you were with Herman last night?" I smiled and giggled. Lillian, Ruth and another lady Sylvia all laughed. "Who's deal?" I asked as we started to play Mexican Train Dominos. Out of the corner of my eye, I could see Ginny moving away from the doorway.

# Chapter 2 – The Zteam

In an obscure building in the capital, the ZTeam came together to discuss the intelligence they had gathered on the missing persons from the community care centers. Simon was wrong. It was way more than 11 centers. There were seven people sitting around the black conference table in the windowless office. One of them was Cliffside Stonewall.

At age 50, Cliff was just starting to gray at the temples. He bore an eerie resemblance to an actor popular in the early 2000s Reggie Coast. He was 6' something with gray eyes that could pierce your mind with their raw intelligence if you stared back at him too long. But his movie star look was due to a botched experiment. To disguise him in a covert operation, he had been given an injection that nearly killed him and left him with this very familiar face everyone seemed to relax around. "So? What's the plan? We need to get somebody on the inside to figure out what's going on and how to stop it," Cliff offered to the group. His rage was at the end of a very short leash.

His boss, Walter Archer, leaned way back in his chair and scratched his bald head. He leaned so far back, Cliff was afraid he was going to tip over. But right at the point of no return, Walter shifted his weight and sat straight up. "I agree. Are you ready for a new mission?"

"Absolutely, sir," Cliff replied. He was in between everything. His daughter was off at college; his wife, actually ex-wife, was in Aruba with a 'friend'; and he either needed to move or renew the lease on his apartment. Weatherby, his dog, had passed a few months ago and his best friend Albert had just gotten married for the third time. Cliff was afraid if he didn't keep moving, he would drop dead soon, like his Dad, who had died at 53 of a heart attack.

"I agree we need someone on the inside. However, to pull that off, you'd have to go undercover at one of those community care centers. And that would mean taking another injection, this time to age you," said Walter as everyone at the table stared at Cliff, waiting for his answer.

"I figured it would come down to that," said Cliff. "Yes, I'll do it." He didn't want them to know he was scared shitless the injection might go haywire.

"Unless you've got somebody else . . ." He turned his steel gray eyes on each one of the team members sitting around the table. They all shifted in their seats and shook their heads no or averted their eyes. One by one, their mannerisms indicated that they all had turned down the job.

"I thought so. I'm your man," he said, inwardly seething that the ZTeam was a bunch of wusses. "Okay. Once I get the injection, then what?"

Walter walked Cliff through the scenario. First the injection, then the waiting. It would probably take three days. Then they would have one of the ZTeam admit him to a care center. They had already picked one out. On the screen behind Walter, the ZTeam had plotted all the centers with missing residents. Walter said, "They were all on ley lines. And there seems to be a big gap here, pointing to the chart. We believe one of these three centers will be next." He rattled off the names, with the last one being the Westchester Community Care Center. "Cliff, your choice."

The ZTeam knew Cliff had hunches that usually turned out to be pretty good. Cliff knew which one to go with. He had gotten the willies when the third center name was said out loud. "The last one, the Westchester Community Care Center. That's where I'll go."

# Chapter 3 – Westchester Community Care Center

We were playing Mexican Train Dominos again when Ginny brought Reese Hardaway into the game room. She introduced him and we invited him to play. Already Ruth was cozying up to him since he was quite handsome even in his late 80s or early 90s. "You look vaguely familiar," she said, adjusting her glasses. She smiled and her gold tooth gleamed.

Lillian stared at Reese and said, "You look like that famous actor. I think he's dead now. But you're a dead ringer for him."

Reese laughed, "Well, the good news is I'm on this side and not on the other."

"Reggie Coast," I said to the group. "You look like Reggie Coast."

"Yeah, I used to get that a lot when I was younger. Now if I only had some of his money," said Reese.

We all introduced ourselves and asked Reese if he knew how to play. In no time, Reese had figured out the game enough that he could make small talk and play. We played for a few hours before the group started breaking up. First Ruth left to meet Herman somewhere. Then Lillian said she wanted to lie down before dinner. Sylvia shuffled off to catch a viewing of a movie in the cinema. Soon it was just Reese and me at the table.

"So, what brought you here?" Reese asked, helping to put the dominos back into the game box.

"My husband Thomas. He needed more care than I could give him at home, so Thomas, his robot Simon and I came here. I dare say my daughter is trying to declare me incompetent so she can take Thomas off all the electronic devices. But I just know there's something coming or something happening that will change things. I keep holding out, but it had better come fast."

Reese nodded. "I understand. I have no family so my niece suggested I try this place out. What did you do before you came here?"

I sighed, "I was a writer. Some fantasy, mainly mysteries, some children's books and a few nonfiction pieces when I first started out. My daughter tells me I'm living in my own time-traveling world."

"Would I know any of the titles?" Reese asked.

"Maybe one. *Monterey Blackhawk*. That was my favorite. The heroine warps into another universe where she is hailed as the champion they have been waiting for. However, she can't remember who she is, but she doesn't believe she is their champion. She suffers from amnesia and can only remember the street signs—Monterey Blackhawk--from where she warped. That's why they call her Monterey of Blackhawk."

"I'll have to look it up," said Reese.

"Better not spend too much time on the reading devices or you may learn we're not safe. You know residents are being abducted from community care centers in the state. I'm sleeping in my clothes at night. You might want to also." I replied. "Well, I best check on Thomas before supper. It was nice talking to you, Reese." I left him staring after me as I walked back to my room.

I was still sleeping in my clothes at night, much to the dismay of the housekeepers. They threatened to call my daughter, but I said "Phooey." She was trying to have me declared incompetent anyway so what did I care. She was going to do what she wanted to do. She always did.

That night I pulled up the covers to my neck and waited, pretending to be asleep. That's when Ginny and another aid came into the room. They put a device on Thomas's wrist. I sat straight up in bed. "You are not taking him without me," I said loudly, struggling to throw the blankets off.

"Now, now, Margaret, you just lie down and fall back asleep," the aid said to me, pushing my legs back onto my bed and trying to pull the covers back over me.

"Stop it!" I shouted. "Stop it!" I pushed the aid's hand away and kicked off the covers for the second time. Just then, Reese appeared in the doorway. "What's the matter, Margaret?" he asked.

"These dang fools are going to take Thomas and I won't let him go without me." Clearly Ginny and her aide were unprepared for the ferocity I was giving them. "Besides I help Thomas with his work. I transcribe his technical papers."

"You transcribe his technical papers?" Ginny asked, repeating what I said as if trying to understand it.

"Yes. Yes. You must take me along," I said.

Reese looked at my outfit. I had my best tan slacks and white blouse on, complete with slip-on exercise shoes. He was standing there in his light blue pajamas and a navy-blue robe.

Ginny really seemed flustered. She repeated to herself, "You transcribe his technical papers?"

"Yes. Yes, I do." Something in Reese's eyes caught my attention. He motioned to himself and nodded his head, indicating that he wanted to go as well. Hiding my shock, I continued, "And this gentleman here, he helps with the research Thomas needs. You must take him too."

Ginny's circuits must have been overloaded because she repeated what I said about Reese, "He helps with the research Thomas needs?"

"Yes. Yes." I was getting frustrated at how robotic Ginny was acting. Or maybe she wasn't acting? I didn't have time to ponder. It was imperative we be given devices like the one Thomas had. I stuck out my arm and motioned to Reese to stick out his arm too. "We must go with Thomas to help him."

Ginny finally nodded her head and pulled two more devices out of her pocket.

I asked, "What happens next?"

"Wait. You must wait. They will find you." After looking at her watch, Ginny and the aide left the room.

"Well I sure as hell don't want to go into outer space with my pajamas on," Reese said. He sprinted out of my room, seemingly like a much younger man. And when he returned, he wasn't even breathing hard, although he had managed to put on a pair of jeans, a long-sleeved pullover and a coat draped over his shoulder. He carried a small duffle bag.

"What's in there?" I asked.

Reese said just stuff and didn't elaborate.

I had already tucked Simon's intelligence chip inside my bra. I had my SpaceTime device in my sweater pocket, which I just had slipped into. We waited. He sat in the corner on the uncomfortable visitor's chair no one ever used because it was hard as a board. I sat on the bed. I so wanted to tell Simon we were leaving him, but I didn't want to risk activating him. He could be pretty noisy when he woke up—and somehow this all seemed like a stealth operation. I did turn on his room camera.

"What are they doing?" I asked, pointing to the hallway.

In his hard chair, Reese was positioned close enough to the door so he could see out by moving his head a bit. "Looks like they are adding to their group of abductees. They split up and are going into certain rooms, probably to slap on these devices," he nodded with his head toward his own arm. The device on his arm lit up. I looked at mine and at Thomas's. They were all lit. And then we disappeared.

# Chapter 4 – The Starship

There were about 30 of us standing in what was reminiscent of an old saloon. I had become separated from Thomas and saw him leaving the room on a floating glass bed. I shouted at the two individuals walking alongside him, "Wait, wait," but no one waited as I made my way to the doorway, which was now closed. An old-fashioned barmaid, for that's what she looked like, stood by the door, blocking my exit. She wore a yellow dress with a hoop skirt beneath, but it was floor length and her top was not revealing at all. I thought of books I had read on the Wild West and her image didn't quite jive with the era.

"Where are they taking him?" I asked. "He's my husband and he needs me."

"Don't worry, Miss. Master Thomas will be back shortly. They are running diagnostics to make sure the teleportation device didn't injure him."

I must have run my eyes over her outfit more than once, for she asked, "My dress? Is it not pleasing?"

I told her saloon girls typically had knee-length dresses or skirts so their colorful petticoats peeked out. And that her top should be sleeveless to bare her arms and shoulders. And she needed net stockings held up by garters.

She turned her back to me for a moment and then turned around again. Her outfit had been adjusted and she looked perfect for the barmaid role.

"Yes, yes. That's more like it," I nodded my head.

"Oh, the introductions are about to start. Please take a seat," she motioned me to a nearby table. Reese was looking for me and I waved him over.

"Welcome aboard our Starship. I am Captain Meno and this is my staff, Ginny, Isabelle, Gavin, McCloud and others you will meet over time. You should all feel special, for you were selected to participate in this historic voyage. I am captain of this Starship. We are headed to Mars where we need you to help us colonize our base there . . .

Captain Meno talked at length about what was needed. The residents from Westchester and a few other community care centers were suddenly animated and asked lots of questions. Robots glided around serving water, juices, coffee, whatever the guests wanted.

I turned to Reese and said, "Boy, this room is getting hot. It should be cooler so we don't all get heat stroke."

Over the din of Captain Meno and the residents, I could hear a speaker in one of the ceiling panels saying, "Hot, hotter, hottest. Cool, cooler, coolest." I pointed to the ceiling but Reese shook his head. He didn't hear it at all.

Soon the room was a comfortable setting again and I wondered what I had just been privy to. The doors opened so we could leave the saloon. I stood up and the yellow-dress barmaid waved to me. Reese got up too and followed me out. We stopped just outside the doorway.

"Thomas is resting comfortably in his chambers. Would you care to join him?" said Aide #1, for that is what her name plate said.

"Absolutely," I replied, suddenly very tired.

Reese said, "I'd like to come too."

Aide #1 nodded and guided all of us to our chamber. "Here are your new quarters. There are three sleeping stations. And a room robot. I hope that is satisfactory."

Reese said, "Woe, I need to be near Margaret and Thomas but not in the same room as them."

Aide #1 responded, "So this is not satisfactory?"

"No, it is not. We need another chamber for me. Margaret and Thomas will share this one" Reese replied.

Aide #1 opened up a display case on her arm and pushed several buttons. She closed the display and then said, "Reese, your room will be here," and pointed across the hall. "Margaret and Thomas will be here," and she opened both our doors.

Before leaving, Reese asked, "Will you be okay?"

"Yes, yes. Suddenly I am very tired. I would like to take a little rest after Thomas gets settled in," I said. Reese nodded and walked across the hall through his doorway, which closed behind him.

"You have a personal robot for Thomas, just like before," said Aide #1. "His name is Nomis. Nomis, here is your charge, Master Thomas, the Ancient One." Nomis came out from his charging port and started fussing over Thomas, just like Simon would.

"Would it be okay if we changed Nomis's name to Simon?" I asked. It would be easier for Thomas to remember." "For Thomas, the Ancient One, to remember," I said, using their terminology.

"Change Nomis's name? Change Nomis's name? Change Nomis's name?" Aide #1 said several times. Finally, as if receiving a response inaudibly she said, "Why, of course. Nomis, your new name is Simon."

Simon responded, "Very good."

To me, Simon seemed much sharper than the Aide. I had a lot to think about. Simon noticed the fatigue setting in and said, "Here you go, Miss Margaret. Sit down here on this sleeper station. I will tend to Thomas. He will be fine."

Aide #1 left us as I sat down, kicking off my shoes. When I laid my head back on the pillow, the sleeper station immediately adjusted its firmness until I was settled in. Then a light blanket was pulled up by Simon. "Sleep well, Miss Margaret. Sleep well."

Although I had wanted to think about all the stuff that had happened today, I just couldn't. I went to sleep almost immediately and didn't wake for what seemed like a long time. The smell of coffee finally roused me. Simon greeted me, "Good day, Miss Margaret. Would you like a cup of coffee?"

As I began to sit up, the bed covers retracted and the back of the sleeper station raised to help me sit up. "Wow, what time is it?" I asked, stretching a bit.

"Just a little after 10 a.m. Eastern Standard Time. Reese has come to the door a few times asking for you. Thomas is fine. I just fed him some breakfast and was waiting for you to get dressed before we took a little walk. I know how much Thomas liked those on Earth."

# Chapter 5 – Aidan's House

In his bedroom, Aidan could hear his momma in the other room talking to his grandmother on the speaker device. "You're kidding, right? Surely, they can't just have vanished?" said his momma, standing in front of the LCD screen.

"That's what the Westchester Community Care Center director said. There are about 15 residents missing from their facility, including Margaret and Thomas," Grandmother said in a voice that seemed ready to boil over.

Aidan came into the room. "What's going on? Great Nana and Great Papa are missing?"

His momma nodded her head. "Yes. It appears they left the Care Center yesterday in the company of about 13 others."

"She said it would happen." Aidan said.

Grandmother spoke from the LCD screen, "What do you mean?"

Aidan responded, "Great Nana knew she was going to be abducted. She just knew it."

"That's absolutely ludicrous. How could she have known?" said Grandmother, snorting at the mere thought. She dismissed Aidan's comments and went on, "The director said they have alerted the authorities and will let us know when they are located. In the meantime, I'd better step up my efforts to have Margaret declared incompetent. Going off on a lark with Thomas and 13 other people certainly is a sign of mental illness that even a judge won't be able to reject." She smiled smugly to herself. "I've got to go." The grandmother's picture got smaller and smaller until it disappeared entirely.

"What do you mean Great Nana knew she was going to be abducted?" said his momma.

Aidan filled in his momma on everything that had happened on his last visit to see Great Nana.

"And you didn't think to tell me?" his Momma asked incredulously.

"Great Nana said you'd all think she was nuts. Judging by Grandmother's reaction, Great Nana was right," Aidan responded.

"Well, we'll have to sit tight to see what the local authorities find out. Perhaps they'll be located quickly and returned to the center. I don't know how long Thomas can exist without Simon taking care of him."

Aidan asked, "They didn't take Simon with them?"

"No, that's what Grandmother had said before you came on the call," his momma responded.

"Humph. I wonder . . ." Aidan was already wondering if Simon might hold a clue.

"Wonder what?" his Momma asked.

"Nothing. I'm thinking if they don't locate Great Nana and Great Papa quickly, I might just go up there and bring Simon home until they are located. I wouldn't want him to go missing too," Aidan said.

"Okay. I guess we could both go up there and see if there are any clues and take home what we need to," his momma agreed.

# Chapter 6 – The ZTeam

"Phase 1 of Cliff's mission was successful," Walter told the team. "He was abducted last week at 0100 hours. His mission now has moved into Phase 2, where he will learn all he can about his abductors, thwart their mission, and return home."

The elite ZTeam around the conference room table looked relieved, thankful they weren't going to be asked to participate in the mission if Cliff had failed. Walter realized Cliff was right. The ZTeam was a bunch of wusses.

"Don't you have someplace to be?" he grouched at everyone. "Get out of here."

As they filed out of his conference room, Walter looked up to the heavens and said, "I hope you can figure this out, Cliff. Everything is resting on you." He pulled out a pen from his top pocket. With a touch of a button, it turned into a smoking stick. He took a deep drag and held his breath, letting the tobacco permeate his lungs. Then he slowly began exhaling thru his nose as he walked out of the room.

The sensors in the conference room came alive, "Smoke, smoke," but nobody was there to hear the warning.

# Chapter 7 – The Blind Tiger

Simon showed me where the cleaning chamber was and laid out some clothes for me. It's amazing how good you feel after a shower. I felt rejuvenated and capable of tackling the world. I'll have to ask Reese if he feels better himself. Maybe they're pumping in oxygen here, just like they used to do at some of those megachurches on Earth.

"Good morning, Thomas," I said as I gave him a big kiss on his cheek. I looked at him carefully, but there was no reaction, sadly no reaction whatsoever.

Simon was watching me closely. "Give Master Thomas, the Ancient One, time to recover, Miss Margaret. You must give him some time."

I sighed. It seems like that's all I have been doing for the last 10 years is waiting, waiting for something. I hope this is the something I have been waiting for, I thought.

"Simon, can I keep my old Earth clothes? I am very fond of that outfit," I said, as I saw him getting ready to drop my clothes down some type of chute in the room. "Thomas's too, if you wouldn't mind."
"As you wish, Miss Margaret. I took the liberty of contacting Mister Reese. He should be here shortly." Just as he spoke, there was an announcement in our room. "Mister Reese is here."

"Open door," Simon said and the door slid open. Simon quickly folded the clothes and put them in a drawer that opened automatically from one of the walls and became invisible once again as it closed.

"Good morning, Margaret, Thomas and, of course, Simon." Reese gave a big stage bow that made Simon say, "Tsk, Tsk," but strangely I could sense the robot was happy.

"Hello, Reese. I can't believe I slept until 10 am. That would have been unheard of back on Earth," I said.

Simon held up a light jacket which I slipped my arms into. "The corridors can be chilly at times," the robot said. He then placed a throw on Thomas, who was now seated in a gliding chair. We all stepped out into the seemingly endless white hallway with light gray tiled floors. Each doorway was outlined with the tiniest hint of charcoal gray.

Thomas led the group, with Simon walking behind him, followed by Reese and me walking side-by-side.

"So how did you sleep, Reese?" I asked, wanting to know if he felt as refreshed as I did.

"Strangely very well," Reese replied. "Look, I wanted to thank you for sticking up for me when, what was her name? Oh Ginny, wanted to leave me behind."

"No problem. I'm glad to have the company. I only hope I haven't gotten you in over your head. They keep referring to Thomas as the Ancient One. It seems he is pretty special to their plans."

"Yeah, I gathered that myself. And no, you didn't get me in over my head. I have had special training for situations like this," Reese replied, but he didn't elaborate, tilting his head toward Simon.

I nodded. I knew he was aware that Simon was listening to everything we said. We'd have to wait until later to talk more.

Thomas and Simon led us back to the saloon, which was now a 1920s blind tiger, also known as a speakeasy. As soon as we entered the room, our clothes changed to appropriate era dress. I had on a flapper outfit, a brightly colored low waisted lemon-colored dress. I was glad I had a jacket which had transformed into an ecru shawl and I patted the intelligence chip still hidden in my bra. Thomas and Reese both had beige lounge suits, with hip-length jackets sporting two large pockets. Underneath were darker beige double-breasted vests with six buttons and two pockets as well, over snappy slacks. Thomas was oblivious to the changes, but Reese reacted with a bit of surprise, as did I.

One of the Starship's crew was the barmaid again, directing us to a table in the corner. Funny, but I thought she removed a "Reserved" sign from it, but I couldn't be sure. I looked at Reese to see if he noticed it, but he had been watching all the activity in the bar. People were dancing, getting drinks, or singing along with the piano player. All this before noon -- tough for me to comprehend. A few people were still in their nightwear. That's when I figured out the clothes from the Starship were nanotechnology, shifting with the environment.

The music stopped and all turned to look at Captain Meno who had entered the blind tiger without any fanfare.

"You all seem so well rested. Again, I want to welcome you aboard our Starship. If you all would take a seat. Yes, yes, you too," pointing to those gathered around the piano player. "I'd like each of the tables to introduce themselves to the room," said Captain Meno.

There were about 50 of us in the room, a few more men than women by my estimation. Ages ranged from 60 to close to 100, judging by the looks of some. I was glad to see some of my close friends from the Westchester Community Care Center there. I waved as Ruth introduced herself and noticed that Herman was with her. When Lillian introduced herself, I was practically giddy. I could see Eddie in the corner near her. Why, we could all play Mexican Train Dominos, I thought. But that's, of course, after we figure out why we were here in the first place.

Captain Meno acted more like a cruise director than a Starship officer. When he looked at me a little more closely than the others, I hoped he couldn't read my thoughts or see the slight outline of the chip in my bra, but he was waiting for me to introduce myself and Thomas.

"Thomas is very special. He's our Ancient One, and you will learn more about what that means during our trip to our destination," said Captain Meno.

When everyone had been introduced, Captain Meno continued, "I know you all have been wondering how to communicate with your families, to let them know you are safe. We have set up a communications center where you will be able to contact your families. If I could have those in the first two tables come forward, we will take you there. "

Magically, table numbers appeared. We had one of the highest numbers, so I knew we would be last. I suddenly became very hungry and realized the only thing I had this morning was a cup of coffee. When the barmaid came over, I asked if I could order some food. She produced a menu from her apron that rivaled some of the best restaurants I had ever eaten at in Chicago. I ordered a Spanish omelet with hash browns and a toasted blueberry muffin. Reese ordered the same as we waited for our turn in the Communications Center.

# Chapter 8 – Communications Center

Just as Reese and I finished eating, our table buzzed. It was our turn in the Communications Center, which was outfitted with about a dozen communication devices. Simon rolled Thomas next to me as I sat down at one of the gray consoles near the back. Reese moved on to locate another terminal.

As soon as I touched the device, it responded, "Greetings Margaret and Thomas. Who would you like to send a message to?"

"Aidan, my great grandson."

"Very good." In just a few moments, his picture appeared. As I talked, the device created a video.

"Aidan, your Great Papa and I are okay, I said. We are on a Starship headed for Mars. As you can see, Great Papa has not yet awoken, but I am very hopeful this is the event I have been waiting for, the one in which Thomas is restored to his former self.  We love you lots! Bye for now."

The device played back the video, making one suggestion. "Instead of saying 'okay,' you should say 'fine.' Okay means satisfactory. Fine conveys in good health."

I was a bit perturbed by the device correcting me. After all, I was the writer, I thought.

The device noted the narrowing of my eyes. "I am sorry I have displeased you. "

I quickly recovered. "No, I was just a bit angry at myself for not choosing the word you suggested.  Please make the change." For some reason, I did not want the device to know it had irked me.

The device made the change and replayed the video. Even though I had said the word 'okay,' the change to 'fine' was seamless. Even my lips matched the word.  The editing was flawless.

The device said, "Thank you, Miss Margaret and Master Thomas. We will send your message when the laser relay satellite is in range again."

"Will Aidan be able to send a message back?"

"I am sorry. This is only a one-way transmission at the moment. When we arrive on Mars, we will be able to send two-way transmissions."

I got up from my chair only to find Reese standing behind me. I looked at him quizzically, but he said under his breath, "Later." I nodded and we exited the room.

# Chapter 9 – Herlehy's Pub

It was a few days before I was able to talk to Reese alone.

I woke feeling even more refreshed, more rejuvenated than the day before. However, as I studied my reflection in the mirror, I could see no physical changes taking place.

The 1920s blind tiger had now morphed into Herlehy's, a 1940s pub. Red leather-topped pedestal stools lined the massive wooden bar. Square wooden tables with even squarer wooden chairs were spaced around the room. Some tables were pushed together to make tables of eight or 12. At a few tables, crew sat listening intently as travelers told stories of long ago, when they were dentists or doctors or contractors in various building trades, judges, ministers, hair stylists, teachers, police officers, or whatever profession they had been in.

Our clothes again transformed, this time into 1940s wear. I had a blue padded blouse with a below-the-knee length beige skirt. Thomas had on a yellow zoot suit jacket with baggy legs. Simon settled Thomas in beside me. We ordered breakfast again, something that was becoming a bit of a routine for us. When our food arrived, mine an omelet, Thomas' a nutritional shake, I told Simon that I would feed Thomas.

"Very good, Miss Margaret. I need to run a diagnostic. One of my sensors is not working properly. I would like to leave for a bit."

"Absolutely, Simon. Take care of whatever you need to. We'll be fine." I replied. As Simon was about to exit, Reese entered wearing a bright blue jacket with matching slacks. Simon motioned to Reese where we were sitting.

As soon as Reese sat down, a barmaid came to take his order. I was about to speak when Reese shook his 'no.' He then reached into his left jacket pocket and pulled out a small device the size of a mechanical pencil eraser. He set it down on the table, waved his hand over it to feel the vibrations, and then nodded.

I must have had a questioning look on my face, because he went right into an explanation.

"I thought we might want to speak freely. Jamming device," Reese said with a nod.

"So, whatever happened in the Communications Center? You seemed to be done pretty fast." I asked in between mouthfuls of my omelet.

"Yeah. Well there was no one to communicate with so I left."

"They didn't pull up your niece?" I asked, a bit puzzled.

"Right. I think they didn't have my niece on video because I wasn't really supposed to be on the spaceship. Remember I was only allowed to come because you said I was Thomas' assistant as you were."

"Why that is true," I said, noticing Simon coming in the door. I motioned to Reese to pick up his device. He put a napkin over it and scooped it up right as Simon wheeled himself to the table.

"Master Thomas, why you finished your shake in record time." Simon said, pausing for a response neither I nor Reese could hear. "Very good. Yes, shall we?" Simon looked at us and said, "Please excuse us. Master Thomas said he'd like to go to visit the holodeck to see the ocean and the sea turtles hatching." With that, Simon bustled Thomas toward the door, waving at us on the way out.

Reese had already put his device back on the table, near the center where a glass vase with a red tulip sat.

"So you never said what you did for a living," I mentioned.

Reese smiled wryly. "You never asked. I worked in the government."

"Well that explains the device. I have to ask. How do you feel when you wake up each morning?" I said.

"Great. Actually, very fit. I don't have the usual aches and pains I had back on Earth. From looking around the room, the others must feel the same," Reese responded, nodding toward Ruth and Herman and Lillian and Eddie who were cutting up rugs on the dance floor. "And you?"

"Right. I feel great too. So how are they doing it? I was wondering if they were pumping more oxygen to make us feel better."

"You may be right, but let's keep our suspicions to ourselves for the moment and watch," Reese suggested, pocketing his device once again before our barmaid reached the table.

"Yes. It was nice dining again with you Reese. You must join Thomas and me any time," I said pleasantly.

"Will do," Reese replied as I left him sitting there. Out of the corner of my eye, I saw him move to the table where Ruth and the other dancers were now sitting and ordering drinks.

# Chapter 10 – Captain Meno

"I just don't like having her on board, Sir," Ginny said, standing next to Captain Meno in the Navigation Chamber.

"Why? Do you have any evidence to back up your comment?" asked Captain Meno.

"No, but. . . ." Ginny replied.

"No buts. The matter is settled. Bring me evidence she is detrimental to the mission. Then I will take action. Until then, we are proceeding as planned," Captain Meno said.

"Yes, Sir," Ginny replied, with a steely glint in her eye.

# Chapter 11 – Herman the Dentist

We had been in space for 14 days when Herman set up shop as a dentist. He had talked to the crew and told them he needed to repair Ruth's cracked crown.

After a short discussion, the crew offered Herman a chamber where he could see patients, Ruth being his very first. Herman found all the necessary instruments needed and a robotic assistant he named Murgadroid.

Ruth told me later, "Dr. Herman was wonderful. I didn't feel a thing. If you have any problems with your teeth, I would definitely recommend him."

I laughed, "Well, it does seem like he is our only dentist."

Soon Eddie asked if he could have a chamber to preach in. Lillian thought she'd like to do nails again and asked Ruth to set up shop with her as a hair stylist.

Deck 3 was transformed into Maxwell Street, with vendors and brightly colored shops all along the corridor, giving everyone an entertaining way to pass time during our voyage. There were even checkerboard tables under the Earth trees Herman had asked to be planted. The crew didn't interfere. Frankly, they seemed relieved we were able to amuse ourselves.

My feet often found their way to the Communications Center where I continued to send messages to my great grandson Aidan and then to Maxwell Street. Thomas would go for long corridor strolls with Simon, eventually ending up in the holodeck watching the sea turtles. Thomas seemed to be talking more to Simon, although I wasn't privy to their telepathic conversations.

For me, I find myself mulling over things, like I wondered if we humans greatly outnumbered the aliens. That's how I spent my days.

# Chapter 12 – Oliver Twist

About six weeks after our abduction, for that's what I called it in my head, we were all asked to go to the bar, which now had been transformed into Oliver Twist, a 1960s bar. A cherry-wood curved bar stood in front of tweed upholstered chairs. Round coffee tables with equally rounded upholstered chairs were splattered around the room. A few print rugs could be found here and there.

Captain Meno greeted us. "Please take a seat. I must share some tragic news." He paused until everyone was seated. To me it seemed rehearsed. "Your home planet Earth was destroyed by an asteroid. I have some footage here."

Suddenly the mirrored wall behind the cherry wood bar transformed into a viewing screen where we could see Earth being hit by a huge asteroid, blowing Earth to pieces. "The force of the explosion was enormous. Nothing remained. I am sorry for all your losses."

Thomas, Reese and I were at our usual table. I burst into tears, "Oh my dear great grandson Aidan. Oh my," I said as huge tears rolled down my cheeks. Reese put his arm around my shoulder.

I turned my head toward Thomas, who just now blinked. "Do you know what this means, Thomas? This means everyone on Earth is dead, everyone, including our great grandson Aidan!" I held my breath, hoping upon hope I would get an answer or acknowledgment from Thomas, but none was forthcoming.

Simon said, "Thomas is deeply upset about Aidan's death."

I stood up. "Please excuse me," I said as I headed back to my chambers. I could feel the eyes from Thomas, Simon and Reese on my back, but I didn't care. I had just lost the one person whom I loved as much as Thomas. It just didn't seem fair. No, it did not seem fair at all.

# Chapter 13 – Ginny

It had been six weeks since Margaret had come aboard. Ginny had watched the friendship thicken between Margaret and Reese, attributing it to both being assistants to Thomas, the Ancient One.

However, she was still convinced Margaret had the capacity to ruin the mission and that wasn't going to happen on her watch.

She decided the next time the conversation between Margaret and Reese wasn't audible, she was personally going to check out their table to see if there was some sort of device there jamming the airwaves.

If she was able to secure such a device, then she'd have the proof Captain Meno needed to take further action, action Ginny knew she'd relish.

# Chapter 14 – Sleeping Chamber

Several more weeks passed. I was inconsolable over the loss of Earth and all its inhabitants, including Aidan. I went through the motions of living, but didn't really care that I lived. I rued the day Thomas and I went on the Starship. We should have been on Earth with our family in our last days.

Simon had taken Thomas for his morning stroll. I was alone in my chamber when I heard a distinct buzzing sound. It was pretty steady as I followed the sound to the wall where Thomas' and my old Earth clothes had been stored. I waved my hand as I had seen Simon do and a drawer came open from the seamless white wall. I followed the sound and reached in to find my SpaceTime device in my sweater pocket.

"What?" I thought to myself. I pushed it on and there was Aidan, smiling at me.

"Great Nana! At last you answered. I have been worried about you," he said.

"You're not dead?" I asked in shock.

"Dead? No, although I must admit my hair looks like crap," he laughed.

"We'd been told Earth was destroyed by an asteroid," I said.

"What? No way! We're all still here," he said, "even Grandma," winking at me.

"Humph. Did you get my communications?" I asked, my suspicions getting aroused.

"Communications? No way! I was hoping you'd send me a SpaceTime message right after you and Great Papa disappeared. I waited and waited until I couldn't wait anymore and decided to contact you."

I briefly told him I had been sending him messages for the first six weeks until we were told two weeks ago that Earth was destroyed by an asteroid. "Now why would they tell you that?" Aidan asked.

"I think I know. If we don't have any place to return to, then we'll make the best of the place we're going to," I said.

I could hear Thomas and Simon just outside the door. "I have to go. I'll contact you soon. Love you! Bye."

Aidan responded with "Love you too, Great Nana. Bye!" just as I shut off the SpaceTime device. I hurriedly tucked it into the drawer and closed it, hoping Simon didn't notice the drawer shutting as he wheeled Thomas in.

I still had my back to the doorway as I pinched my cheeks to make them puffy and look like I had been crying again.

Simon looked at me carefully. "Miss Margaret, you really should take a walk to the holodeck to see the sea turtles. It will do your soul wonders."

What does a robot know about souls? I thought.

As Simon settled Thomas into his sleeping chamber for a short nap, I thought about his suggestion. "Maybe I'll see if Reese is available for a walk."

"Jolly good, Miss Margaret. Master Reese was down on Maxwell Street playing checkers when Thomas and I walked past him earlier."

# Chapter 15 – Sea Turtles

I found Reese exactly where Simon said he would be. He was playing checkers with Eddie.

"Reese, would you like to come with me to see the sea turtles?" I asked.

He looked up at me strangely. I indicated with my eyes for him to come with me.

"Sure. Just let me finish this game with Eddie. Hey, you and Lillian want to come?" Reese asked.

I was a bit disappointed that he asked them to come along, but I made a good show of it, "Simon tells me it will be good for my soul."

"Really? He said that about your soul?" Eddie asked, being our designated minister now.

"Yes, he did. I was surprised myself," I said.

As soon as the checkers game was over, Eddie, Lillian, Reese and I headed to the holodeck. It took a few tries before we got the right program to start. Simon was right. My soul seemed to breathe again as we took off our shoes and walked along the shore line in the sand. We could see some tracks where baby sea turtles had hatched and made their way back to the ocean while other nests were staked out with flexible fencing on three sides.

Eddie and Lillian made their way down the beach from us. I asked Reese if he had his jamming device. He shook his head 'no,' but walked us closer to the crashing waves.

"The water acts like a natural jamming device. What's up?" Reese asked.

Taking a deep breath, I said, "I heard from my great grandson Aidan."

"Heard from him? Heard from him where? How?"

"Aidan gave me a SpaceTime device before we left Earth. It went off this morning. I spoke to him just before I found you playing checkers."

"You mean Earth is not destroyed?" Reese said evenly.

"Not by a long shot. Plus, Aidan never received any of the taped messages from the Communications Center. That was all show."

Reese picked up a stone to skip in the ocean. He whistled low and his eyebrows were all scrunched up.

After a long pause, Reese asked, "Okay, so where's the SpaceTime device now?"

It's hidden in the pocket of the sweater I took from Earth. I had Simon keep our old clothes."

"Okay. Don't let Simon catch you talking on the device. When you do talk to your great grandson, do it where water is running, either in the shower or by the ocean, okay? That will keep them from hearing your conversation. And whatever you do, don't tell anyone. Not even Thomas. Best for him to think Earth is still destroyed. The crew would kill to keep that information quiet."

Reese skipped a few more stones before he spoke again. "Look. I just might want to borrow your device. I'd like to get in touch with some of the people I work with."

"Work with?" I asked.

Worked with," Reese said smiling. "I've been feeling pretty good lately so I forget everything is in the past."

"Yes, it is or so it seems," I said, mulling over Reese's slip of tenses. Maybe he's not what he seems himself. Maybe none of us are, I thought.

# Chapter 16 – Sleeping Chambers

Disaster waited for me upon my return from the holodeck. Or perhaps I should say near disaster.  Upon opening the sliding door, there stood Simon, Ginny and Captain Meno along with Thomas in his gliding chair. They all stared at the SpaceTime device in Simon's hand.

"Oh Miss Margaret, I was just showing them the device you had in your hands upon my return," Simon said matter-of-factly.

I tried not to let my face show how nervous I was. I hoped they could not sense my racing heartbeat. If they did, I would say I had been running in the sand along the ocean in the holodeck.

"Oh yes, I had forgotten all about it. I turned it on earlier to see if it still worked," I said.

"Yes. I told them I thought you were talking into it," Simon said.

"Maybe talking into it are not the right words. I was merely repeating the instructions my great grandson Aidan had told me so I could turn on the device."

Ginny smiled insincerely. "And just what does the device do?" She took the device out of Simon's hand and turned it over and over, examining it.

"Why it's a game," I replied levelly.

A game?" Ginny repeated, not quite understanding the term.

"A toy," I said, waiting for them to process that information.

After a few moments of uncomfortable silence, Simon responded, "Toy--an object or thing for a child to play with."

Captain Meno reached for the device and then asked, "So what does this toy do?"

Praying silently the gaming portion would turn on first, I asked, "May I?" Captain Meno nodded as I took the device from his hands. Deftly I touched the switch on the side just to make sure it was still in the correct position. It was.

I turned on the device and various multicolored puzzle shapes flashed across the screen. "The idea is to build an object fitting the puzzle shapes together." With a few flicks of my hands, I built a flower vase. It was crude, but the screen showed it was functional, rating my efforts accordingly.

I tried to hand the device back to Captain Meno to try, but he shook his head. "We shall leave you now. I am sorry for the intrusion," Captain Meno said as he walked toward the door.

Ginny walked behind him. If she had had a tail, it would have been tucked between her legs.

When the door closed behind them, I asked Simon what they had thought the device was originally. He said when he first told Ginny about it, she seemed to think it was some type of transmission device.

I must have cocked my head funny because Simon continued. "Because I heard you speaking into it, Ginny thought it was a talking device."

I nodded my head. "I'm sorry I didn't show it to you earlier. I was trying to remember all the instructions my great grandson had told me about it. It must have seemed like I was speaking to it when I was really just talking aloud, remembering."

"Yes, humans do strange things when trying to remember," Simon agreed.

Thomas was looking at the device. Simon nodded his head in silent agreement, saying, "Yes, it's a toy to build things."

I was extremely grateful neither I nor Aidan had shown Thomas the device, for surely he would have told them, in his logical fashion, exactly what it was and how it worked. In his past life, he had designed many things and created schematics, technical theses, and many videos, books, presentations, and drawings showing just that. However, Thomas always felt his crowning achievement was his work on artificial intelligence.

In 2025, Edison Rocketry launched a space probe manned by AIs. Their mission had been to propagate and terraform Mars. Communications failed shortly after landing on the Red Planet. The ZTeam suspected sabotage. The American people knew even less, attributing its failure to a crash landing on an unforgiving planet.

# Chapter 17 – The Shimmer

Ruth was the first to exhibit the shimmer. She was pretty proud of it. She'd open her mouth wide and point to the tooth Herman had replaced the old crown with a new one. The crazy part was she'd try to talk to you while her mouth was wide open and her finger was in it.

Gently I grabbed her hand and pulled it from her mouth. "Oh, Ruth, I do see the tooth. Yes, it does have a shimmer to it." We were in Oliver Twist celebrating Ruth's birthday.

"I think it makes her mouth look kind of sexy," Herman said. He smiled his crooked smile at Ruth and blew her an air kiss.

"You don't think it should be removed?" I asked. "Maybe it's some sort of infection?"

"Heavens to Murgadroid!" Herman laughed. "No, I had a robotic assistant, the best one I've ever had, humans included, and I've had some very good ones. That's not an infection. The best I can come up with it's something in the crown compound interacting with her saliva. It seems harmless. She's had it for a few days now. No temperature. No night sweats. And I've taken another image just to double check."

"Humph," was all I could respond with.

"To the birthday girl, Ruth," Herman said as he raised his drinking glass.

"Cheers," I responded with a pasted-on smile as we clinked glasses.

"Salut," Reese said as he joined in the festivities.

Ruth blushed and made a big deal about smiling with her mouth open so we could all see the shimmer.

Just two days later, Lillian showed us her shimmer. She had had Herman recap her two front teeth. The way she smiled, you'd think she had two buck teeth.

All I could muster was, "That's nice, Lillian," as we once again were sitting in Oliver Twist.

When Lillian left the table to go to the restroom and reapply her very red lipstick, Ruth went with her and I slid over next to Herman.

"You still don't think this is a virus, do you?" I asked Herman quietly.

"Ssssh. If the patients think it's a virus, it'll put me out of business," Herman said with the air of someone who had made and lost fortunes in the past. "What are you so worried about? It's only a chemical reaction," his white teeth matched the white of his shirt collar as he smiled at me.

The jukebox blared a fast song from the 1960s. Herman pulled me out on the dance floor before I could say, "No." I shook, twirled and twisted, all the while watching the ladies' room door for Ruth.

Just as Ruth came out, I waved at her to cut in. She'd taken to smiling with her mouth open a bit wider than it should be.

I was ready to duck out as soon as Ruth cut in, but as I turned to leave the dance floor, Reese was behind me, asking "May I?" The music had turned to a slow, bluesy number.

There was so much I wanted to talk about, but Reese scrunched up his eyes as if to say, "Not here," so I closed my mouth and enjoyed the moment. Reese was a very good dancer, I thought, and when he looked at me, he made me feel like I was the only woman in the room.

We sat back down. My heart was racing. I attributed it to the dance I had with Herman. At least that's what I told myself.

It was about a week later when Reese found me on Maxwell Street talking to Ruth, Herman, Lillian and Eddie. "Let's go see the sea turtles this afternoon." Reese said.

The others begged off, saying they were just about to head back to their chambers. "Go ahead, you two," Ruth said laughing.

Is that how others see us as 'you two' I thought, for that wouldn't do. After all, I am married to Thomas and even though I have never done anything for Thomas to question my loyalty, I wouldn't want the perception of others distorted. I waffled on whether I should go.

Reese smiled and asked again, "Sea turtles?" I could tell from his eyes he had something to tell me.

My hesitation vanished. "Sure."

Once inside the sea turtle program, we could see from the tracks in the sand that Thomas and Simon had been here earlier.

"Good," was all Reese said as he walked me to a far end of the beach, away from the doorway. He took off his shirt.

I thought, good grief! He thinks there's more to us just like the others, I said, "No, no, I'm married," pushing him away.

He grabbed my arm and said, "I know you're married. Look." His eyes traveled up his muscled right arm. He patted his right shoulder. There was a partial name 'Ian' and just two digits '20'. What remained of his tattoo had taken on a shimmer. "I need you to laser what's left. I've been working on it in my room now for a while." Reese pulled a laser pen from his pants pocket and some alcohol pads.

"You want me to remove your tattoo?" I repeated back to him, just to make sure I had heard what he said over the crashing surf.

"Yes. I've got the shimmer. Whatever the shimmer is, I don't want any part of it. The tattoo needs to be removed."

"You want me to operate on you here? Without any anesthetic?" I said all wide-eyed like a two-year-old child in a candy store.

"I don't want anyone to know you lasered it out. I brought a flask and a piece of wood to bite down on. It'll be like the Old West." Reese tried to reassure me. "Whatever that shimmer thing is, I don't want anything to do with it. My shoulder feels prickly, like there are things crawling underneath the surface."

51

Reese was looking at my face, which must have had a huge question mark on it. "It's my niece. Her name is Breelan and she was born in 2020," Reese answered the question in my head.

"Beach chairs and suntan lotion," I said loudly. Two white Adirondack chairs materialized along with a bottle of lotion. I dragged them nearer the water. "Okay, take a swig, get out your wooden stick, and lay down on your stomach facing the doorway. I'm going to sit on this chair with my back to the door. "

"What's that for?" Reese asked, pointing to the suntan lotion.

"I'm going to put a blob on your back now. If anyone enters the holodeck, let me know and I'm going to swap the laser pen for the suntan lotion and start spreading the blob out. You'll need to hide the piece of wood you're using between your teeth."

The lasering took much longer than expected to break down the metallic color globules into smaller ones so his white blood cells would eat them. I had just finished when I heard splashing in the water. I was so intent on lasering I hadn't noticed Reese had passed out. I leaned over to pull the stick out of Reese's mouth and said, "Wake up," in his ear. I started spreading the lotion on his back when Herman and Ruth walked up, followed by Ginny.

"Hi Margaret. I should have known you would still be in the holodeck with Reese," Ruth laughed. "He's not bad to look at you know, for a man his age."

Herman said, "Yeah, we were thinking of playing dominos tonight and wanted to know if you and Reese wanted to join us. Then we'd have eight. We could meet in Oliver Twist around 7:30 pm." We still used Earth time references to stay oriented in space.

Ginny walked over to the far side of us and looked closely at Reese's back. She could see where the blob of suntan lotion had been because the rest of his back was red, including where I had lasered his tattoo.

Ruth asked the question, "What's the white blob on your back, Reese?"

"Reese sat up and began putting on his shirt. "Shrapnel. It never tans. Been that way forever. Dominos sounds good for me. What about you, Margaret?"

"I'd like to check on Thomas first, so I may be a little late, but sure. Sounds like fun." I replied.

We both stood up. The Adirondack chairs disappeared along with the suntan lotion.

Ginny looked at both of us and then smiled, "Very good." She turned to leave. Herman and Ruth followed, holding hands.

Keeping close to the water, I whispered to Reese, "That was close."

"Yes. I am so sorry. I guessed I passed out from the lasering," Reese said.

"Here's your laser pen," I said, grabbing Reese's hand just as Ginny turned back to look at us.

She gave us a pasted-on smile or was it a smirk? It was hard to tell at this distance.

# Chapter 18 – Extras

Reese was right. The shimmer was not something you wanted. It seemed just about everyone in Oliver Twist had it. Anything metallic seemed to attract the nanosites, for that's what Reese had dubbed them. Tattoos with their metallic ink were particularly prone to the creatures, but also artificial knees, hips, breasts, dental implants, you name it, the nanosites were attracted to them.

The lasering was successful and Reese said his shoulder felt fine, no weird prickling underneath the skin. Luckily neither I nor Thomas ever had any tattoos or joint replacements. But that left us with a different type of problem, maybe not so much for Thomas because he was their Ancient One, but for Reese and me. We no longer looked like the rest of them because they had all taken on a shimmer, which grew exponentially.

For Ruth, first it had been her tooth, then her breasts.

"Why Ruth, you never told me you had breast implants," I said to her one day in Oliver Twist when her cleavage was particularly noticeable. It was obvious the shimmer was there as well.

Ruth just gave her wide-open-mouth smile, winked at me and said, "Some things are best kept secret."

When Herman came up to the table, I noticed he had an extra digit growing from his pinky finger.

"Herman, what in tarnation is that?" I asked.

"Funny, but one night my hand was tingling. The next morning, I noticed this little bump. Being the scientist that I am, well really a dentist but still a man with a scientific bent, I thought I'd wait to see what happened. It wasn't but a few days later that another digit popped out. It's been enormously useful in the dental office, so I decided to keep it rather than laser it off," Herman said matter-of-factly.

Ruth asked, "Have you felt any tingles, twinges?"

"Oh yes. My knee has been feeling tingly," I replied.

Reese walked up to the table just as I replied to the question, "Really?"

"Yes, yes. I wasn't too sure what to make of it and was thinking of going to the infirmary but since you both said it's normal, I won't worry about it," I replied.

"What about you, Reese? Have you felt any tingles?" Herman said, wiggling his new pinky finger around so Reese could see it.

Reese never missed a beat, "Why yes. I've had some twinges in my shoulder. So, you're saying that's normal?"

Herman and Ruth both looked at each other and then turned to Reese and me, saying in unison, "Why yes."

I wondered just when their smiles started to look like Ginny's?

"Sea turtles?" Reese asked.

"Absolutely. The waves, the ocean, the sea turtles all help my internal clock. I sleep much better when I walk along the ocean," I replied.

"Herman, Ruth, interested in coming?" Reese asked. I secretly prayed they would stay away. "No, we're going to hang out here for a while," Herman said.

Once in the holodeck, Reese and I headed straight for the ocean.

"What the heck?" I asked, never finishing my sentence.

"See, I told you the shimmer was not a good thing. I'm sure the nanosites are rewiring the humans somehow. I'm hoping when you said your knee was bothering you it was a lie. Otherwise we'll have to take the laser pen to it."

"No, I lied. But did you notice how Herman and Ruth smiled just like Ginny. It was only with their mouths, not with their eyes. I think they have a massive infection of nanosites."

"Agreed. We're going to have to come up with something to make us shimmer," Reese said. "Otherwise they will figure out we're not infected and it won't be pretty."

Reese skipped a few stones into the water. I mulled over the problem and then said, "Makeup."

"What?" Reese asked, "What did you say?"

"Plain old-fashioned makeup. We can have the replicator create some shimmering talc. Then we just need to dust ourselves before we go out each day."

"Brilliant," Reese said and kissed me on the forehead. "I don't know what I'd do without you. You have been an asset to me since the very beginning."

My forehead tingled from his impulsive kiss. I wondered just what that meant?

# Chapter 19 – Thomas

We'd been on the starship for three months. Thomas and Simon were out so I decided to try on my old Earth clothes. They were very baggy. I guessed I had lost maybe 30 pounds, going from a size 14 to a size 8 or 10. I also felt young, as if not only the weight had left me, but the years too. I was definitely going to have to discuss this new development with Reese.

I had managed another message to my great grandson Aidan. As Reese instructed, I took the SpaceTime device into the shower. Then I kept the device out to play a game when Thomas and Simon returned.

Funny, but it seemed like Thomas was trying to talk to me. I could see it in his eyes.

Simon said, "It won't be long now. Soon he'll be able to talk to you so you can hear him."

I nodded, wondering what this new development would bring.

Our shimmer talc worked. Herman and Ruth just smiled when they saw Reese and me shimmer.

# Chapter 20 – The Great Deception

Meeting Reese in the holodeck after Thomas and Simon had already been there became a regular thing for us. There we could discuss whatever new discoveries we made as we tried to unravel the mystery of our abduction and captors.

Others on the starship felt it was a miracle or salvation to be rescued from a miserable death by old age in the Community Care Center. We were convinced there was much more to the agenda than was being revealed.

"Reese, have you tried on your Earth clothes lately? Mine are incredibly baggy, like I've lost weight." I asked Reese.

"Funny you should say that. I had the replicator make a tape measure. I've lost several inches off my waist."

"So, what do you think is going on?"

"I think we are reverse aging. Let's see if we can trick the holodeck into revealing what we really look like now. Holodeck, make the ocean calm so the sea is like glass," Reese commanded.

Suddenly the ever-churning Atlantic Ocean slowed to a rippling tide. We slipped off our shoes, rolled up our pants and walked into the water, trying to catch a glimpse of ourselves in the gently undulating ocean.

There it was. The sunlight was just right. "Oh," was all I could manage. I looked as I did when I was in my 60s. I was about 30 years younger. So, Reese was right. We were reverse aging.

I looked at Reese's reflection. He was still in his 80s.

"Oh," Reese said, putting a finger to his lips to signal not talk. Grabbing my hand to walk back to the shoreline, he then commanded the holodeck to return the ocean to its previous wave pattern.

We walked a bit more hand-in-hand before I realized we shouldn't be. I dropped his hand and turned to face him.

"What's going on?" I asked.

"We are reverse aging, or at least you are," Reese said. "I'm afraid I haven't been entirely truthful."

"Don't tell me you have the shimmer!" I said anxiously. "I don't know what I would do without someone to talk to."

"No, I don't have the shimmer. Let's walk along the sand, farther away from the door." We walked slowly as Reese began to explain. "I am part of the ZTeam sent to investigate the abductions."

"ZTeam?" I asked.

"Elite government security force."

"So, you wanted to be abducted?" I asked, trying to get my brain around what Reese was telling me.

"Yes, I was sent to the Westchester Community Care Center to be abducted *if* there was an abduction, which there was. And you helped me get onboard the starship by saying I was Thomas' research assistant."

"To blend in with the residents, though, I had to take an aging injection, which is why I still look like I'm in my 80s. But I could see from your water reflection that you are younger. I'm going to have to fix my problem and it's going to take your help."

"So, you're not in your 80s?" I said, befuddled by his admission that he was much younger than he looked.

"Correct," Reese said evenly, realizing I was having trouble grasping the idea that he purposely aged himself to be admitted to the Westchester Community Care Center.

After a long pause, I said, "How old are you really?"

"I'm 50." Reese admitted.

"Married?" I asked, for suddenly that seemed important.

"No. Divorced."

"And the name on your shoulder?"

"My daughter, not my niece."

"Well, I guess you must think I'm a cougar," I said with a weak laugh, finally seeing the irony in it all.

Reese didn't laugh. He stopped walking which in turn made me stop. He looked at me intently with his steel gray eyes. "I don't think that at all. You're my friend. And right now, I really need one. I have a reverse aging injection but I need someone to watch me after the dose has been given. I may be prone to seizures."

"What do I need to do to help you?" I said, trying to forget about all the information he had just laid on me.

"Well, you'll need to spend the night," Reese said.

"That's one heck of an invitation," I said, turning away from him.

"Look at me," Reese said, pulling at my hand to turn me back around to face him. "I really need your help. "

I took a deep breath even though I knew my answer already and said, "Okay."

Reese continued, "I've been thinking about this. Everybody thinks we're sleeping together anyway so it won't seem abnormal if you're seen entering my sleeping chamber one evening. You'll need to tie me down, give me the injection, pretend to have sex with me and when I calm down, untie me."

"Good grief, our first night together and we're already into S&M," I said, "You do have a dark side to you."

Reese searched for the humor in my green eyes. Finally finding it, he slowly smiled, "You're right. It will be a night to remember."

"I just hope it won't be like the Titanic, memorable but fatal," I replied.

# Chapter 21 – The Injection

Two nights later, after Thomas and Simon had fallen asleep, I slipped my lavender robe over my silk pajamas which I wore over my underwear.

"Thomas, please forgive me. I'll explain everything," I silently said to myself as I padded along the hallway in my slippers to Reese's room.

Knocking lightly, I heard Reese call out, "Enter." He stood by the door and greeted me with a cinema kiss. I was surprised by his ardor, but played my part perfectly, throwing my arms around his neck. We knew we were being watched, particularly in the hallways.

Reese had positioned his bed in the far corner. He indicated with his eyes where he thought the room sensor was located and pulled me close for another kiss. He wore blue and white checked pajama bottoms with a light blue T-shirt. Even in his 80s, he was ruggedly handsome. I only hoped I looked equally attractive.

As if reading my mind, he said loudly, "You're beautiful," and turned his head toward the sensor discreetly as he wrapped his arms around me.

"Oh Reese," was all I could think to say at the moment. Not much of an actress.

He laughed, which broke the tension a bit. "That's all you can say?"

I tried again, "Oh Reese, you are very special to me."

Reese cocked his eyebrow, "Just special?"

"Very special," I murmured, nuzzling my nose into his chest, and hugging him tightly.

"Much better," Reese said playfully, taking my hand and leading me to his bed.

"I like it rough," Reese announced and pulled out the cloths we'd be using to bind him.

I helped him take off his shirt. He had a nice physique: broad shoulders, patches of gray hair. I took a minute to look at the shoulder where I had lasered his tattoo off. It was still red, like a dull sunburn, but no letters, no wording, no shimmer. I kissed it. His skin was hot and tasted salty.

Reese helped me take my robe off, kissing me on the forehead, and then in the crook of my neck. He then slowly unbuttoned my pajama top.

"What's this?" Reese laughed as he saw my bra. "Underwear too?"

"Of course," I said with a smile. "Just the way you like it." I playfully slapped him on his bottom with one of the cloth ties.

As I worked to tie him down, his whispered in my ear. The injection is in my pajama bottom pocket. You should give me 10 ccs of the drug. That's so I don't reverse age too quickly. Once you give me the drug, put that piece of wood over there in my mouth. Then get on with your play lovemaking. It'll probably take about an hour before my thrashing stops. Once that happens, you can untie me and leave. You know I really appreciate your help."

"I know," I said, pushing him down on the bed. Once he was secure, I pulled up the sheet to cover us so I could find the syringe in his pajama pocket. Rats. He didn't tell me where to inject it.

"Where?" I whispered.

"In my pocket," Reese responded.

"No, I have it. Where do I need to inject the solution?"

"Deltoid? No, how about the vastus lateralis?"

"Where?" I asked,

"Top of my leg. In the muscle."

"Okay," I said as I pulled the covers over my head and scooted down. I pulled off his pajama bottoms and nearly laughed in relief to see he too had boxers on. I carefully wiped the injection site with the alcohol pad he had, inserted the needle and delivered the dosage. Then I recapped the syringe and stuck it back in his pajama bottoms, throwing them to the floor as I shook off the covers from my head.

Reese's eyes were closed. "Good grief. I hope I didn't kill him," I thought.

His eyes snapped open, but he wasn't there. His eyes were brutally cold and he started thrashing. I barely had time to slip the stick between his teeth before he started roiling.

I did my best to give the room sensor a show, kissing him, rubbing him, pretend hitting him. I was sure to keep the sheet over me when I straddled him and began moving my fanny up and down like a rabbit, although in reality I was a bit higher in position. Picking my movements to match his and then eventually giving up on the rabbit motions, I could then just lay next to him, waiting for his breathing to return to normal. By the time he quieted down, we were both sweaty. Removing the stick from between his teeth, I put it on his nightstand.

"Did you enjoy it?" I said loudly (by now I was an old hand at this acting thing) as I untied him.

"Immensely," Reese said with a weak smile. When his second hand was untied, he rolled enough to hug me and said, "Thank you." He kissed my forehead.

I got up off the bed, put my pajamas back on over my underwear, slipped into my robe. I turned to say goodbye, but Reese was fast asleep.

"Typical man," I said, smiling to myself. Somehow that seemed to make it all okay.

# Chapter 22 – Strike Pocket

Reese and I visited the calm waters on the holodeck about a week later. He definitely was younger. Maybe in his early 70s. I now looked like I was in my late 50s.

"Now who's the cougar?" I asked Reese quietly, before the holodeck returned the waters to their normal waves.

He laughed. We headed to Oliver Twist, which had morphed into a 1980s bowling bar, The Strike Pocket. It was an exact replica of one Thomas and I had frequented many years ago, when we bowled after work with a great group of friends.

I walked over to the corner to check out the pinball machines. They were identical to the ones Thomas and I had spent many hours playing. Reese headed to the bar to order a couple of beers.

It was at that moment Thomas walked in, followed by Simon. And I do mean Thomas walked in. He was upright, looking mildly confused, maybe amused by the decor of the bar. He walked up to the bar, stood next to Reese, introduced himself as Tommy, and ordered a beer.

"You're Margaret's husband, Thomas?" Reese asked.

"Margaret? I'm not sure. Thomas is my name, but my friends call me Tommy," was all he responded. Thomas then took his beer and sat down at our usual table. Simon hovered over his left shoulder.

As I approached the table, Simon blocked me. "Thomas has just returned from the other dimension. He needs time to get acclimated. Later, please." Somewhat dumbfounded by Thomas' upright appearance, I could only manage a nod and left the bar. Reese followed my departure with his eyes, then turned back to Thomas, who was taking everything in, running his fingers over the wood chair back. A few others came over to talk to Thomas, but Simon deftly shooed everybody away.

Reese whistled slow and low under his breath. This was a humdinger, he thought. He drank his beer and ordered another. It was going to be a long night, he thought, as he continued to watch Thomas- Tommy.

# Chapter 23 – Tommy, the Ancient One

I waited for what seemed like hours for Thomas to return to our sleeping chamber. When he did walk in, he turned to me and asked, "I've seen you before. Who are you again?"

"Of course, you have seen me before, Thomas. I am your wife Margaret." I started to get up from the chair I had been sitting in to finally hug him, but Simon shook his head, so I remained seated.

"Wife? I am flattered, but I have no wife," Thomas replied, looking at me strangely. He then turned to Simon and asked, "Am I to share a place with this strange woman?"

"No, Master Thomas. We can move you to a separate unit," Simon said as he packed up a few personal items Thomas had.

Remembering his manners, Thomas said as he was leaving, "It was nice meeting you, Margaret."

I cried. No, I sobbed so long and so hard my face was one big blotch of red. I went in the cleansing chamber and sobbed some more as the water pummeled me from all directions. When I felt I couldn't cry any more, I lay down on my sleeping station and fell asleep from sheer exhaustion.

The next morning, I looked around the room. It seemed oddly sterile with Thomas' few items removed.

What happened to him? How come he doesn't know me at all? I was at a total loss.

It was a while later when I heard Reese at the door, "Margaret, are you all right? How about if you let me in?"

"Open," I commanded the door from my chair. Reese walked in breezily.

"Are you all right? He looked at me steadily as I tried to hold back the tears.

"Yes, I'm fine," I replied, my eyes still glistening.

"Liar," he said. He pulled me up to my feet and gave me a great big bear hug. I broke down and sobbed into his chest. He just kept rubbing my back saying, "There, there."

When I finally stopped shuttering and heaving, he said, "Let's go see the sea turtles." His eyes looked at the room sensor.

"Okay. Let me just rinse my face and put on some powder," I replied. When I reappeared, I asked, "Do you think I should bring my sunglasses?" I was wondering just how red my eyes were.

"Absolutely. It's going to be quite sunny today at the beach," Reese said as he handed me my sunglasses. I put them on and we exited my sleeping chamber.

# Chapter 24 – The Reveal

On the holodeck, Reese ordered the waves to be somewhat strong so we could talk anywhere.

"So what happened?" Reese asked.

"Thomas doesn't know me. When I first saw him in The Strike Pocket, he seemed unsure of himself, like a child exploring his surroundings. Simon shooed me away, saying he had just returned from another dimension. However, when Thomas returned to our sleeping chamber, he still didn't know me. He had no idea he was even married," I said in disbelief.

"He introduced himself as Tommy, not Thomas. Does that give you any clues?"

"He called himself Tommy when he first got out of college before he started working. What did he order to drink?"

"He ordered a BB," Reese said. When I looked at him quizzically, he said, "A Bonnie Blue beer."

"He did?" Why that's what he drank long before I knew him."

"I think he regressed to an age before he knew you," Reese said. "When did you first meet?"

"Thomas was 29 when we met in 1983. By then, he called himself Thomas and drank Higgins beer."

"My guess is Thomas regressed to age 25 or 28, before he met you. For him, you don't even exist and he's definitely not married."

"Ouch," was all I could say.

"Think back. What were some significant events he told you about before you met? Who was he dating? Where was he working?"

"He was dating Patty back then. He had started at the company where his dad worked as a technical writer. Later he would become an engineer for the firm. He played softball, liked a few rock bands and a country singer from Maywood, and drank Bonnie Blue. Oh, and he bowled and played pinball. He was a decent guitarist and he could sing."

"Is there anybody here named Patty?" Reese asked.

"Not that I know of, but I haven't met everybody," I responded.

"Okay. So why do you think the aliens want Thomas?"

"Well, they called him 'The Ancient One' so they think he's someone special."

"Special enough to advance their cause, whatever that is," Reese answered. "Well since we both were brought along because we are his research assistants, we'll have to let him know we're here to help him. That way we'll have access to whatever he's doing for them."

"Right, although it won't be easy working beside him and him not knowing I even exist," I said.

After a long pause, Reese said, "I can't even imagine what it's like for you, so I won't pretend to. But I do know this. We need to stick with him. We won't be able to figure out what's really going on unless we do. Hey, do you still have that communications device? I'd like to borrow it to reach my ZTeam boss."

"Yes. Hopefully Thomas and Simon didn't take it when they moved out yesterday."

"They moved out? You didn't tell me." Reese said.

"Yes. Thomas still didn't recognize me and asked Simon if he had to share a room with me. Simon said 'no' and they moved to another sleeping chamber."

"Wow. Like a knife in the heart," Reese said.

"Or an injection in the leg," I replied with a twisted smile.

"Now *that* does hurt, I can attest to that," Reese laughed.

# Chapter 25--TAO

Our fellow travelers took to calling Tommy "TAO," short for The Ancient One. Reese and I were given another table to sit at in The Strike Pocket. Whenever Tommy entered the bar, new friends would be invited to sit with him. First there were Ruth and Herman with the six fingers. Then Lillian and Eddie joined him. Pretty soon everybody in the bar had a chance to talk to Tommy.

Reese and I were some of the last to sit with Tommy.

"I've met both of you before," Tommy said, looking over us with his sea blue eyes.

"Yes, I'm Reese. We met at the bar the first day you walked in. And this is Margaret."

"Hello Thomas," I said.

"Thomas," he laughed. "You sound like the teachers in Catholic school. I'm Tommy."

"Tommy, nice to meet you." I said not trusting myself to say any more. I was afraid I'd start crying.

"What do you do?" Tommy asked us.

"Both Margaret and I are research assistants. If you find yourself needing assistants in the future, we'd be glad to help you," Reese said.

"That's very kind of you. I'm not working on anything at the moment but I just may have need of your help in the future. I'll keep that in mind," Tommy said. "Now, are you interested in a game of pinball?"

"Sure. I'm not so good at it, but I'll give it a try," Reese said. He poked me with his elbow.

"I love pinball. I might be a bit rusty, but I'll give it a shot," I said.

We ordered round after round of beer. I'd drink a few sips and conveniently lose my drink. Reese did a better job of keeping up. I had forgotten Thomas-Tommy, could drink when he was in the mood. In the end, although we did lose every single game to Tommy, we did keep them close enough to be interesting. Tommy liked that. I could tell. When the band started playing, Tommy decided he'd had enough and went to sit down to listen to the music.

The band was the Classical Durples. I hadn't heard them before, so Reese and I hung around at the bar for a few songs. They could play anything, from country to blues to rock. Their lead singer was a woman. I almost choked on my beer when the band introduced her as Patty. I looked over at Tommy. He was mesmerized. I knew how this was going to end even if Tommy didn't.

# Chapter 26--Doppelganger

I was sick. I had a rash circling more than half of my torso from my back to my right side. I was pretty sure it was shingles, just another remnant of the chicken pox virus. The rash made it difficult to sit, to lie down, to shower, even to stand and walk. I felt so under the weather I stayed in my room for nearly a week. Waiting for my rash to crust over, I took zinc and B12. I rubbed oil of oregano where I could reach and waited. Odd but Reese never came to see me. In fact, nobody did. I felt strangely abandoned.

When I finally felt fit enough to emerge from my self-inflicted cocoon, I headed to The Strike Pocket and arrived just in time to see someone who looked like me disappearing into the ladies' room.

As if on cue, Reese walked over to me. He'd been hanging out by the pinball machines with Tommy. "How're things?" Reese asked. We had developed a code phrase a while back. "Peachy as a nectarine," I responded.

He smiled and kissed me on my cheek. I was surprised by this unusual display of affection. Pretty much he kept a tight lid on things. "Let's go see the sea turtles," he said. Tommy piped up. "I love the sea turtles." So the four of us, including the ever-present Simon, headed to the holodeck and spent some time walking around. Tommy was well versed on the sea turtles. He could tell us their habits, their life expectancy, etc.

Simon said, "Master Tommy, it's just about time for band rehearsal.

Tommy nodded and started to dump the sand out of his slip-ons, which he had taken off to walk the shoreline. I looked up at Thomas, a bit taken aback. I knew he had played both the guitar and the violin and could sing. What I didn't know about was his interest in being in a band, but then I remembered that Patty was the lead singer. It was all coming full circle.

Simon asked, "Master Thomas, aren't you forgetting something?"

"Oh yeah," Thomas reached into his shirt pocket and handed me a folded piece of paper. "I know you thought you were married to me. I thought you might feel better if that chapter was closed."

"How do you know how I feel, Thomas?" I shouted at his back. He turned to say, "It's Tommy, Margaret. It's always been Tommy, not Thomas. And I am sorry."

Reese stood in front of me and held me by my forearms. "Margaret, Margaret, Margaret, look at me," Reese said.

I looked at Reese and then at the piece of paper in my hand. Reese let go of my forearms. I unfolded the paper. It read "Tommy and Margaret are not married." It was signed by Eddie, our minister.

A big tear rolled down my cheek. "So that's how it all ends? In six words?"

"Let's walk," Reese suggested, and so we did. We walked close to the shoreline, sometimes getting sprayed by the waves, other times skirting the receding water. We walked for a long time. Reese waited for me to break the silence, which I did eventually.

"Well, I guess --in reality--I cannot fault him. He regressed to an age earlier than when he knew me," I sighed.

Reese said, "That may not be exactly true. Since he felt it necessary to write those six words tells me you remain in a slice of his old memory. And it's in conflict with the new memories he is making now, which is why *he* needed to close this chapter. So where does this whole band thing go?"

"Well, he eventually hooks up with Patty and they stay together for a while."

"And then what? When did you come on the scene?" Reese asked.

"Well, funny but I don't remember what the timeline is now. Could my memory have been altered too with that piece of paper?" I asked. "Anything's possible, I suppose. Maybe that's why it was so important to give it to you -- so that memory in your brain would dissipate. So where were you for the past week?"

"I had shingles, my diagnosis. I was pretty sure that's what it was. I had the replicator provide me with some B12 and zinc and oil of oregano. I guess I was a bit surprised you didn't stop by to check on me though." There I had said it out loud. I admitted I missed Reese's company. I hope he wouldn't start acting all weird because of it.

"Well, you won't believe this but you have a double," Reese said.

"A double?" I said, surprised by his admission.

"Yes. Thank goodness we developed our code phrase. She looked just like you. In fact, you might have seen her going into the ladies' room when you came in to The Strike Pocket."

"Funny, but I did notice somebody who looked like me from the back entering the ladies' room. Did she ever emerge?"

"Well, we left pretty soon after you arrived but I'm betting she emerged as either one of the staff or another individual who was laid up."

"What was the giveaway she wasn't me?" I asked.

"When I asked how she was doing, she answered 'Peachy like a peach,'" Reese replied.

I suddenly felt light-headed. Reese noticed how ashen I had become and ordered a couple of Adirondack chairs. We positioned them just outside of the ocean spray so we could continue to talk without being heard.

"There was another me?" I blew the words out from my lips like a leaky balloon as I stared at the water.

"Yes." Reese responded, watching me intently.

Turning toward Reese, I asked, "Why? Why did they send a copy to pretend to be me?"

"You mean the doppelganger?" said Reese. "They might have wanted to test how good their technology was. And it was good. There wasn't anything I could see that they didn't replicate. You were a perfect copy."

"But why copy me?" I asked.

"Why not copy you? You are or rather were an important person in Tommy's life. And I think they were hoping to get me to talk," Reese said.

"How so?"

"Well the doppelganger asked me to go visit the sea turtles. Once I realized she was not you, I decided to go along to see where this little charade was going. She even asked me to raise the waves, but I never talked when the waves were high. I pretended we just liked seeing the force of the waves on the shoreline."

"So why didn't she get the code phrase right?"

"Well, I think it's because the computer system is based on logic. It's illogical to be peachy as a nectarine, so the computer system 'corrected' the phrase to fit its logic."

"Do you think the ultimate goal is to replace the humans on Earth with doppelgangers?"

Reese thought about it for a moment and then answered. "I don't think so. That would take a lot of resources. But the doppelgangers could be targeted for key positions, like our President and the cabinet. And then eventually the heads of other countries around the world."

It was my turn to think about things. "Okay, so how close of a replica was she to me?"

Reese answered quickly, "She was an exact replica."

"Could you tell she wasn't human?"

"It's scary to say this, but I could barely tell, and I've had training. If we hadn't established our code phrase, I could have blown our cover."

I suddenly felt very chilled and quickly ran my hands up and down my arms to warm me. But the friction did little for the cold which lingered and seemed to emanate both from my heart and the ache it felt from Thomas as well as from my head and the revelation that the aliens had a much bigger agenda than we had envisioned.

# Chapter 27—The Communications Device

Reese had asked me for the communications device. I had forgotten all about his request until he reminded me. But when I looked, I couldn't find it. I looked everywhere. Where in the heck could it be? And then I remembered Simon packing up Thomas' things when he moved out. Perhaps he took the device as well.

I asked the replicator where Thomas was. He was in his room so I headed there.

"Margaret, what a pleasant surprise." Tommy said. "Won't you come in?"

"Hi Tommy. Why yes, I'll come in," I said. It was evident he was back in the 1960s. His room was filled with rock posters. He even had a black light on one wall.

"Wow, this is pretty authentic," I said.

"Glad you like it. I decorated it with some help from Simon," Tommy offered.

"I was wondering, Tommy, when you moved out, did you take my puzzle game by accident?" I blurted out.

He looked at Simon and then back at me. "Yes, I'm sorry. I did take it. I thought I could build another one."

Simon reached into the drawer and produced a box. In it were the pieces to the communications device.

"I'm afraid I started the project before all my memory came back," said Tommy. "But I'm willing to put it back into working condition. It just may take me a while."
My heart sank, but my voice never wavered. "It's okay, Tommy. It was only a game. I'm happy to try to fix it. It'll give me something to do.'

Simon parroted, "Something to do. A purpose."

"Yes, a purpose." I responded. I took the box and left, heading back to my room. I met Reese along the way. He was just leaving Maxwell Street.

"My puzzle toy," I said loudly as I shook the box.

He grimaced and nodded.

"Thomas-Tommy, took it apart before his memory had fully returned. He offered to rebuild it but I told him I'd try to fix it. It will give me a purpose."

"Well, I can try to help you too. That will give me a purpose also," Reese said loudly. "Let's go to my room. I may have some tools that can help."

First Reese laid out all the parts on the table in his room. Then slowly he'd move them around until he could figure out where each one fit in. It reminded me of a jigsaw puzzle, which Thomas and I would pour over for hours. As I leaned over, I noticed Reese had a little stubble growing and he smelled like musk. Suddenly very self-conscious, I ran my fingers through my hair more than once.

We ate dinner together in his room as we discussed which piece was next and gave our reasoning for placing this one there rather than that one. When the last piece was put in the device, we looked at each other and finally smiled.

Making sure the switch was on for the game portion, I turned it on. Nothing happened. No lights. No sounds. Nothing. It was a bitter disappointment.

"I'm bushed," I said. "Tomorrow? I can't even think straight at the moment."

"Tomorrow will be fine. It could be something as simple as a crimped wire."

"Yes, or even a battery that needs recharging." Reese added. He walked me to the door and held it open. I pecked him on the cheek, "Goodnight, Reese," I walked across the hall to my room, aware Reese continued to watch me until I finally closed my door. Once in my room, I closed the door and leaned up against it. I was trying to make sense of my feelings.

# Chapter 28—The Cats' Meows

Things were getting strange. The men were frequently involved in arm wrestling in The Strike Pocket, with groups of women huddled around the men, making gentle purring sounds.

Lillian and Ruth asked me to join their Sewing Circle. They were going to make aprons. Now why on Earth or Mars or wherever we were would we need aprons? I couldn't imagine a use for them, but Reese encouraged me to join, just as he participated in the feats of strength with the other men.

Lillian's apron had small pieces of furry fabric sewn on top like dewdrops. It was in complete contrast from the white aprons my mother used in her kitchen. Those had some red or green piping and a pocket for essentials such as potholders or recipes, but basically they were pretty spartan.

Ruth's apron was gawdy by my account. Hers had strips of denim hanging loose. I followed suit and made mine with triangular cutouts of white and gray fabric. When done, all the ladies modeled their aprons while we oohed and aahed. And then Ruth and Lillian turned their aprons around so the front was now in the back, covering their rears. Everyone tittered and let out soft moans, almost like purrs. I tried to mimic them, but I didn't have a clue what I was doing.

Once we all had our aprons in place on our derrieres, we headed to The Strike Pocket to parade around the men. They stopped their arm wrestling long enough to give out low whistles and catcalls.

The very next day the men decided to have a bowling tournament to declare the winner (or winners) whatever the case may be. We headed to the holodeck to watch them compete, with the ladies periodically getting up from their seats to dust some imaginary item off their chair and shake their fannies at the bowlers at the same time.

When that was over, the men decided to have a softball competition the following day. Again, we all met in the holodeck and watched the men compete on various levels of prowess. The ladies again spent time going to the concession stand, dropping things like napkins, and making a big display of picking them up with some rump-shaking going on.

For days on end, the men set up various tournaments to best each other. After arm wrestling, bowling and softball, there was the pinball tournament, then weight lifting and boxing--even a drinking competition. I couldn't imagine what was going on.

"Reese, they're acting like cats in heat," I said aloud while we were looking at the sea turtles. For once, there wasn't a competition in the holodeck, so we took advantage of it. "I don't know what to make of this."

"You nailed it. They are acting like cats in heat. I think that's exactly what's going on here," Reese replied.

"Seriously? It all seems so ludicrous." I replied.

"I think the computer's logic is screwed up." Reese replied thoughtfully.

"You may be right. When we first came on board, I heard through a speaker, 'Hot, hotter, hottest. Cool, cooler, coolest.'" I said. "It's like the temperature regulator was learning."

"Really? Well then, I'm probably right. Somehow the computer has crossed humans with cats and everyone who has the nanosites is now responding to that programming."

"Egad, really?" I said, worrying a bit about what was in store.

"We'll have to play along. Whatever you see them doing, you should do. We absolutely don't want them to figure out we're not infected. That would be very bad since we don't know what their ulterior plan is."

"I guess you're right," I sighed. All this espionage stuff was wearying. I was looking forward to becoming myself again.

"By the way, I read *Monterey Blackhawk*," Reese said. "I liked it a lot. I can see a little of your reluctant heroine in you, you know."

"Oh, I wrote it so long ago. I started it when I was in my mid-thirties. I was going strong and then suddenly life got in the way. I didn't pick it up again until about 15 years later." I replied.

"Well, I liked it. And if Monterey never gave up, you can't either. You've got to hang in there. We'll figure what the aliens are up to." Reese replied.

"I guess," I said not so enthusiastically. "Even if we do figure out what they're up to, how are we going to stop them? And will we ever be able to return to Earth, I wonder."

Reese grabbed me by my shoulders, "Look at me, Margaret." He put his hand gently under my chin and lifted it up so I had to look at his steely eyes which suddenly seemed very warm. "We're going to figure this out. You have to trust me on this. And then I'm going to get you home, to Earth."

A single tear trickled down my cheek. He wiped it off with this thumb.

"I forgot to tell you," he said. "With all the cats' meowing, it slipped my mind. I was able to get the communications device to work. I couldn't get it to contact the ZTeam but it did connect to your great grandson Aidan "

"Aidan?" I parroted back.

"Yes, Aidan. I told him you were fine and who I was. I asked him to get in touch with Walter Archer at the ZTeam office. I gave him a code phrase to share with Walter so he'd know the message was really from me." Reese responded.

"And you told him I was fine?" I wanted to confirm Reese had communicated that to Aidan, for I knew he would fret when I wasn't on the device.

"Yes, yes. To be honest, he was very suspicious at first and threatened to beat me up the next time he saw me if anything had happened to you. I assured him I was taking good care of you and promised the next time we talked I would have you with me."

"Oh good," I smiled, feeling my heart lift a bit knowing that Aidan knew I was fine. "How did you get the device to work?"

"Old school. I cleaned all the contacts with an emery board from the replicator. I told it I needed to file my nails." Reese gave a lopsided smile.

"Well, since we're revealing things, I forgot to tell you that the day after we had worked on reassembling the communications device, Simon approached me. He asked me not to say anything about the broken device. He kept on saying Tommy tried to put it back together too soon, when his mind wasn't fully restored, but the way Simon said it made me think it was more than that. I don't think he wanted Captain Meno and Ginny to know about Tommy's failure."

"That is interesting," Reese said.

# Chapter 29 – The Communications Device

Aidan was surprised to see a stranger on the other end of his Great Nana's communication device. It was even odder to learn the stranger on the other end was Reese, part of the elite ZTeam. What in tarnation had his Great Nana gotten into? Aidan thought.

Reese assured him Margaret was fine. He didn't seem to say too much about Great Papa Thomas, but Aidan thought that might be because he was still in his deep sleep.

Reese gave Aidan a series of instructions to contact Walter Archer at the ZTeam headquarters to let him know they were safe.

Aidan took a deep breath before dialing the number Reese gave him.

"Walter here," the gruff voice on the other end of the communications device said. "Who is this?"

"I'm Aidan." Aidan replied, taking a big swallow. He could only imagine how intimidating this fellow would be in person.

"Okay, Aidan, how did you get this number?"

"Reese gave it to me. He wanted you to know he was okay and on a spaceship headed to Mars with my great grandparents."

"Okay, Aidan, and what makes you think I'm going to believe you?"

"Well, Reese figured you'd say that so he gave me a special code phrase to use—Zebra Zulu Xanadu."

There was a long pause. Aidan was just about to repeat the code phrase again when the gruff voice on the other end of the line said, "Aidan, I'm going to send a ZTeam member to bring you to our office here so we can talk in a secured environment."

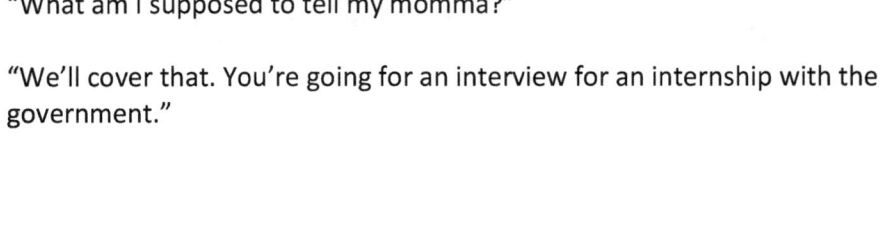

"What am I supposed to tell my momma?"

"We'll cover that. You're going for an interview for an internship with the government."

# Chapter 30—The Internship

Whoever Walter Archer was, he was as good as his word. The next day a man in a black suit named Buzz MacGregor showed up on Aidan's doorstep waiting to escort him to the capital. The man explained to his parents that Aidan had applied for an internship with the government so he'd be gone for a few days for the interview process.

His mother practically purred when she heard he was interviewing in the capital. She didn't have the usual barrage of questions she had whenever he went out with his friends.

There was another fellow, Cassidy, waiting for them in the car. No first name, no last name, just Cassidy. He was their driver who dropped them off at the O'Hare Airport gate where the private planes take off. Aidan wanted to take a few pictures to post online but sensed that wasn't the right thing to do.

Buzz was a huge hulking man, maybe 6'6" tall, about 250 lbs., and looked like he could bench press more than that. His arms were as big as thighs and his dark brown eyes looked like they could see right into your brain.

Aidan decided to busy himself with his communications device until they boarded. Soon Cassidy joined them. He was about the same size as Buzz. Bookends, Aidan thought—and I'm the book.

The trip to the capital was uneventful. Aidan actually fell asleep for a while and hoped he didn't snore or, worse yet, drool, but the two bookends didn't seem to notice. They were busy playing a game of gin rummy over in the corner.

When they landed, Cassidy got the car while Buzz and Aidan waited. Not a lot of conversation between them. Finally Buzz said, "First time to the capital?"

Aidan said, "Yes."

Buzz laughed, "Well, don't expect to see too much. I'm sure Archer will keep you pretty busy until your return."

Aidan didn't find that the least bit funny. It wasn't funny at all.

Cassidy handled the driving with ease, deftly shifting lanes whenever the traffic slowed. Buzz sat stone-faced next to him. Aidan mused that they knew each other so well they communicated with grunts and facial twitches. When Buzz finally said something to Aidan, he had to ask for it to be repeated. Aidan was so deep in his own thoughts he didn't hear the question the first time.

"We're going to run through this burger joint. What do you want?" Buzz said.

Aidan really wanted a plain hamburger with catsup only but figured somehow that would be put him on the wuss list. "What are you guys getting?"

"We like the WhattaCheeseburger Basket. The cheeseburger comes with lettuce, tomato and onion on the side. Great curly fries or onion rings. And a drink." Buzz said.

Aidan breathed a sigh of relief. "That's fine." He could suffer through the cheese. "Fries are good. Catsup too for the fries. And a lemonade to drink."

"Lemonade? Humph. Sounds good. I haven't had one in ages," Buzz said.

Cassidy ordered three baskets. Aidan guessed the ZTeam members must have been as hungry as he was for nobody said a word in between bites. But then again, Cassidy and Buzz didn't say much in general.

Soon they arrived at the ZTeam headquarters. The guards at the gate checked both Cassidy's and Buzz's IDs. They looked at Aidan, "Who's the passenger?"

"Aidan Neath, from Chicago," but the way Buzz said it, the city sounded more like She-kaw-go.

"You got any ID kid?" one of the gray uniformed guards asked.

Aidan pulled out his driver's license. The guard scanned it in. "Son, would you mind stepping out of the car?"

Nervously, Aidan glanced over at Buzz.

"It's alright, kid. They've got to light you," replied Buzz.

"Huh?" Aidan responded, crap, now he was talking like them.

"They have to check you for weapons."

Aidan stepped out of the car while the guard closely looked over his driver's license, comparing the picture with Aidan's face. He grunted. Then he pointed a device that looked like a pen into Aidan's eye and then back toward the barcode on his license. The other guard motioned for Aidan to step forward and put his feet on the indentations in the ground. As soon as Aidan did, a light box appeared near his feet and moved upward, until it cleared his head. Then the box disappeared and the other guard grunted.

"Ok, you're cleared. Here kid," the first guard handed Aidan back his license. He opened the back door of the car for Aidan to get in. As soon as the second guard pressed a button in the guard shack, the ditch disappeared, and the first guard pounded on the roof of the car to indicate to Cassidy to drive forward.

Aidan found himself letting out a whole bunch of air, like a balloon being deflated.

Buzz turned around and laughed, "You ain't seen nothin' yet, kid."

Inside the building, Aidan had to repeat the whole exercise, complete with standing on the indentations so the light box scanned him again. His backpack went through a similar process. Finally, they were heading toward the elevator.

When the gray elevator stopped at the fifth floor, they got off and walked down the gray and white tiled floor toward the third door on the right. Aidan counted things when he got nervous and boy was he nervous. He was ready to make a mad dash out the door.

Buzz knocked on the door and then entered. Archer was sitting at his desk, waiting.

"I heard you had arrived," Walter Archer said in his gruff voice.

Aidan cringed. Walter was even more imposing in person. He too was a hulk of a man, although he had a bit more girth than the others, like he'd spent a lot of time behind a desk now. He had Ben Franklin glasses halfway down his nose. His blue eyes pierced the room. His hair was thinning.

"You Aidan?" Walter shouted.

"Yes sir." Aidan responded, glad his voice sounded level even though he was shaking on the inside.

Looking at Buzz and Cassidy, Walter said, "I'll let you know when he's ready to go to his hotel."

They grunted, almost in unison, and left.

Walter stood up and walked over to Aidan to shake his hand. Aidan was surprised but Walter was actually shorter than him. "Nice to meet you, kid. Name's Walter Archer. Have a seat." He motioned to a stiff-looking gray chair in front of his sleek black desk

Walter walked back to his own chair and sat down. "Tell me exactly what Reese said."

At last a question Aidan had prepared for. Putting his backpack down by his feet, Aidan did as he was told. He sat down and repeated word-for-word what Reese had told him to say.

"And how is it you could communicate with Reese when I haven't been able to?" Walter said, raising his eyebrows.

Aidan went on to explain how he had given his Great Nana—Margaret--a SpaceTime communications device when she had told him she and his Great Papa—Thomas--would be abducted.

"She knew?" Walter asked, tilting his head a bit. His brown no-nonsense eyes were boring holes into Aidan's head. Walter played with a writing stick on his desk, turning and flipping it over and over and over again.

"Yes. She told me a bit before they were abducted. I didn't want to believe it at first. I thought she might be writing another one of her books and was just testing the plot line on me. Turns out she was right."

"So, exactly how did she know?" Walter asked.

"Well, the staff came during the night and identified Great Papa by saying 'This one.' Great Nana wasn't going to let them take her husband without her and so told me that."

"You got any proof of any of this?"

"Yes. Well, at least I think it's what you're looking for," Aidan said as he reached into his backpack and pulled out the intelligence chip from Simon.

"What Great Nana had read online was when the other people were abducted, they'd leave everything behind. Thomas' robot Simon was still in their room. He'd been keeping my Great Papa alive for the last 10 years. My folks and I had to go to the Westchester Community Care Center to clean out their room, so I brought Simon home."

"And?" said Walter, looking at the small device Aidan held out in his hand. "That isn't a robot."

"Right, but it's the next best thing. It's Simon's intelligence chip. I told my Great Nana how to make a similar chip to smuggle it on board. She and I discussed how she might need it to power another robot." Aidan leaned forward in his chair and handed the chip to Walter who had now put the writing stick between his teeth and was clenching it very hard.

Talking out of one side of his mouth, Archer shouted to the air, "Bring me a robot that'll fit this chip." He held it up.

Within just a few minutes, a robot knocked on the door.

"Whatcha hanging out there for?" Enter. Enter," Walter shouted.

This robot wasn't anything Aidan had seen before. It was shaped like a human, but completely transparent. Everything was visible, all its hardware.

"Can you play this intelligence chip? Just from the last say 10 minutes."

The robot took the chip and placed it in a device in its arm. After a momentary pause, the robot said, "Mister Archer, the camera module was activated. I shall play it now."

The robot directed its arm toward one of the walls in Walter's office, the one with no pictures hanging on it to interfere with the images.

The chilling scenes of the abduction of Margaret, Thomas and Reese played out before their eyes.

"Good grief, the actual abduction took place in a matter of seconds, actually 30 to be exact." Walter went back to flipping the writing stick on his desk. "Anything more on the intelligence chip, kid?"

"I don't know. I only watched the end, pretty much what you just saw."

"You did good, kid, real good. I'd like to keep it for analysis. Okay? I'll have our robot make you a copy." Within a few minutes, the robot was handing Aidan another chip, "Here you go Master Aidan. I am sorry for your loss."

"Sentient," Walter said when he noticed the raised eyebrows on Aidan's face. "Not my idea. I like them without feelings. Makes it easier all around."

"You got any plans after college?" Walter asked Aidan.

# Chapter 31 – Whiskers

The whole cat phenomena went on for a while. I found myself bumping and grinding with the rest of them. Poor Reese. He was always the object of my affections. But I didn't know what else to do. Actually, there wasn't anything else I could do. If I didn't play the part, the aliens would know both Reese and I were not affected by the nanosites and somehow that seemed like a bad thing, a very bad thing.

Did you know that cats curl their tongue backwards to lap milk? I even tried that, although I wasn't as successful as the other women. One time in the hallway, Reese grabbed me and kissed me so hard I thought my socks would come off. For a brief moment, I was worried he too had been infected, but then Ginny walked by saying good morning to us.

I did notice that Thomas-Tommy-Tao, whathaveyou, didn't seem to be affected by the nanosites. There must be a reason for it, I'm sure. Patty, though, was definitely affected, but Simon was able to run interference and keep them separated. It seemed important to Simon to keep Thomas away from her during this time. It made me think that nanosites could be transmitted through more ways than Reese and I had imagined.

Finally, the cat calls, wallowing, and rump shaking stopped. The ladies stopped wearing their aprons and the men stopped having their physical contests.

# Chapter 32 --The Dream

I didn't know what was wrong with me. I surely wasn't going to let Herman the dentist examine me. I was afraid he would infect me with nanosites to fix whatever ailed me. And I wasn't having any of that.

Reese saw me in The Strike Pocket. After our usual greeting, he said, "What's the matter with you? You look like something the cat dragged in, no pun intended."

I shook my head, managing a feeble smile. "I haven't a clue what's wrong, but I feel lousy. Maybe it's just a virus?"

Reese looked around and said, "Ssssh. You don't want them to think you're ill. Then for sure they'll know you're not infected by the nanosites."

"Well, what do you suggest? I'd just as soon go back to bed and sleep." I replied.

"Why don't you injure yourself?" When he saw me giving him the crazy eye, he said, "Drop something on your foot so you have to rest. Maybe that's not so good. How about twisting your ankle or pretending to? I can then help you back to your quarters or mine and take care of you until you're better."

"Great idea." On the next song, Reese and I headed to the dance floor and I faked a sprain.

Herman rushed over to see if he could help, but Reese deftly scooped me up in his arms and carried me off, calling out over his shoulder, "Just a sprain. Some ice should do it."

Herman shouted after us, "Yes, RICE: rest, ice, compression, and elevation."

Reese took me to his quarters where he laid me down on his bed. By this time, I was sweating profusely. He asked the replicator for some electrolyte beverage, which Reese handed to me. I drank what I could. Reese kept watch, placing and changing out wet washcloths on my forehead every 30 minutes or so. He asked the replicator for some fever reducer, which he had me take every four to six hours, or whenever he could wake me.

I was in a deep sleep, so deep my astral body was free. First, I saw my deceased dad on the ship's Maxwell Street. Harry wore a red flannel shirt over work pants. His shoes were shined, just like I remembered them. His gray head was thinning which made his ocean blue eyes all that more piercing. I wanted to tell him all about Reese, but he shook his head, telling me instead that he didn't know life was so short. "So short compared to what?" I wanted to ask. But instead we hugged, and he vanished in my arms. I continued to roam the spacecraft. I wandered into Thomas' room. He wasn't there. I floated into The Strike Pocket and saw various groups of people talking. Herman and Ruth were smooching it up in the corner. Lillian and Eddie were on the dance floor. Thomas was playing in the band, with Patty singing lead.

I floated to the Communications Station but nothing going on there. There was no one to contact since we had all been told Earth was destroyed. Only Reese and I knew differently. There was no past for any of us, only an unknown future.

I found my way to the Control Deck. Nothing too exciting there either. Just a few crewmates monitoring the computers to keep us on course for Mars. I wondered where Ginny was. She was always checking up on me. Now's the time to turn the tables, I thought to myself.

Suddenly I found myself face-to-face with Ginny in one of the corridors. She looked like she was talking right to me, but actually she was talking to whoever was behind me.

"How should we proceed, sir?" Ginny asked.

"Proceed?" Captain Meno asked.

"Proceed with Tommy. Should we release the information to him for his review?"

"Absolutely." Said Captain Meno. "Why the hesitation?"

"I am unsure if the information will remain confidential if both Margaret and Reese are his research associates."

"Has Margaret or Reese shown any subversive signs?"

"No, not at all."

"So, what's your point?" Captain Meno asked.

"Well, I'm afraid they might be acting."

"Is that even possible with the nanosites present?"

"No."

"I don't see any reason not to move forward with our plan. Give Tommy what he needs to review before we land. And bring me proof if you see any subversive signs in Margaret and Reese and we will extinguish them."

"Yes sir," Ginny responded and left.

The captain turned as well and headed back to the Control Room.

I woke up, startled to find myself in Reese's bed.

"How do you feel?" Reese asked.

"Better, finally. Thank you for nursing my . . . ankle . . . back to health," as Reese having his back to the room monitor, pointed at my ankle and then at the monitor so I wouldn't say the wrong thing. I so wanted to tell him what I had dreamt or seen in my sleep. Somehow, every word seemed true.

# Chapter 33—An Aqueduct

It was a few days later when Reese and I were finally able to make our way to the hologram deck. As soon as the waves were crashing all around us, I told him about my vision, dream or whatever it was.

"Mmmm," was all Reese managed to say initially. After we walked a bit more on the beach, he said, "Do you think you could have another out-of-body experience in the future? I'd like to learn what Tommy knows now that they're releasing new information to him."

"I'm not sure. I've had a few experiences in the past. Once I was in Hawaii and visited the Iao Valley on Maui. I lagged behind the group I was with to take some pictures of the ancient trees. It was then that I heard calls from the cliffs, like I had stepped back in time. My camera malfunctioned, the battery was drained and I couldn't take any pictures, although it had been working just before then. That night, as I dreamt of ancient Hawaiians, my astral body floated above the bed, or so Thomas told me later. The Hawaiians were welcoming me back, like I had lived there before. When my husband shouted at me to stop it, my astral body fell and jolted me awake.

"Another time I was in my bedroom and sailed out of the window. Higher and higher I went, connected only by a thin, silvery cord. I soon found myself looking down at Earth from outer space. And then, just like that"— snapping my fingers for effect—"I awoke in my bed, wondering if it all was a dream."

For the next few nights, I tried to have an out-of-body experience. I tried drinking before I retired, meditating, reading, walking, you name it. Nothing seemed to trigger one. I finally asked Reese the next time we were watching the sea turtles what he thought of just asking Tommy if he needed any research done. Maybe he'd just tell us.

"I say go for it. We need to find out what he knows."

And so, I did. The next time I saw Tommy in The Strike Pocket, when he wasn't singing or playing pinball, I asked, "Tommy, Reese and I are available to help you with whatever projects you might have. What can we do?"

Tommy took a long swig of his beer and then pulled on his beard a bit. "Funny you should ask. I've just been given some information on the Mission on Mars. Perhaps you could research various ways to build an aqueduct."

"Ok. Do you know the distance or what types of materials might be available?"

"Neither. But you could start by looking at soil composition." Tommy started to get up. "Sorry, can't talk more. My gig is starting." He headed to the stage and gave Patty a knowing nod, the kind of nod that says I'll see you naked later, I imagined.

Reese poked me in the side. "Stop it," he said, noticing where I was looking. "Imagining them naked together will get you nowhere. I know. I used to sit outside my ex-wife's apartment and watch her lover come and go. Archer found me there one night. He told me you can't go back. He said, 'Regrets will eat you up. They distort the past and destroy the future, leaving you in the abyss.'"

I turned my back on them. "I guess you're right. He doesn't even remember he's forgotten me." I wiped a tear away.

Reese pulled up my chin and kissed me hard and long. "Hope that helps you forget what you lost," Reese said with a smile. His steely gray eyes seemed soft, not so piercing at that moment.

Behind me, Ruth and Herman were clapping. Herman walked over and whacked Reese on his back. "Don't know what took you so long to kiss her, Reese! She's a mighty fine filly."

Ruth came over and just said, "Oooooo," showing off her sparkling nanosite teeth.

"Good grief," was all I could think. They were all acting like a bunch of teenagers. Reese headed to the bar with Herman, while Ruth continued to dazzle me with her teeth, grinning like the Cheshire Cat.

"How is the handsome man in bed?" Ruth asked, licking her lips while her eyes watched Reese's backside.

"Ruth!" I said as the red creeped up my face.

She just laughed and said, "Your face says it all. I imagined he'd be that good and I was right!" Ruth left me sputtering as she walked up to the boys at the bar. She put her arm around Reese's shoulder briefly, then let it slide down so it brushed past his rear. She was not above copping a feel whenever and wherever, I thought to myself. Reese turned his head to look at his backside and she dropped her hand. Ruth turned her head now to wink at me.

When Reese returned to where I had sat down, he handed me a beer and took a long swig. He raised his eyebrows and blew out some air between his clenched teeth. "You have no idea how prying Herman can be, and all those intimate questions coming from a minister. I had a devil of a time avoiding any answers that would embarrass you." Reese took another long drink from his beer.

"Actually, Ruth was no better. Obviously those two have an active imagination."

"Imagination nothing. Ruth was giving me a pat down."

I laughed. "Yes, I saw her. What you missed was her winking at me behind your back." Now it was my turn to take a big swig.

# Chapter 34 – The Big News

A few days later we were all called to The Strike Pocket for an update from Captain Meno.

"Greetings Earthlings," he said. The group tittered. Meno in his white uniform smiled broadly. Ginny leaned over and whispered to the captain. Nodding, the captain started over, "Greetings travelers from Earth. We are nearing the Red Planet and should land within the next 24 hours."

The group broke into applause, war whoops and cheers at the news that our destination was in sight.

Captain Meno motioned with his hands to quiet down. "We're landing in the Grand Canyon or Valles Marineris as you would know it. If you look at the screens in the center of your tables, you'll see your cabin assignments and the name of your cabin mate. Quarters are much smaller on the Red Planet, but I am sure you will find them fully acceptable." Ginny and her crewmates fanned out into the crowd.

The screen flashed my name with Tommy's. I momentarily took my eyes off the screen and the next time I looked, Reese's name was with mine. Reese spoke low and said, "I was hoping we'd be paired. Otherwise, I was going to ask to change." I nodded, just as Ginny came up to our table.

"Do you find your cabin mate acceptable, Miss Margaret?" Ginny asked with fake politeness.

"Yes, Reese will be an acceptable cabin mate," I replied, copying how others responded to Ginny or her crew when asked the question. She nodded. "Good, good." And looked at me a long time before moving on.

Ginny returned to Captain Meno and nodded. The other crew members stood behind their captain. "For the most part, you will be confined to base. However, should you need to venture outside, you'll be provided with the necessary protective gear and breathing apparatus. With the terraforming we have introduced, the planet's temperatures in the valley are stable, although cooler than other locations on the Red Planet.

In the holodeck, Reese practically exploded. "Well that explains the aqueduct. Because of the low atmospheric pressure on Mars, liquid water cannot exist except at the lowest elevations and only for short periods."

"Where would they get the water?" I asked. I had taken off my shoes and was digging a hole in the sand with my toe.

"Well, from what I've read, there are two ice caps at the poles. Maybe they're going to melt a portion of one? Or tap into underground ice? Now that seems more logical."

"So, Tommy's task and now ours is to figure out how to move the water from its source to our base camp?"

"Right. My guess would be the spacecraft does not have an unlimited supply of water, or maybe we are using it faster than our captors expected. In any case, I would guess a water source will be our first priority."

"Don't you think whoever settled Mars before us would have taken care of this?" I asked.

"That may be the issue. Maybe they didn't. Maybe they were supposed to, but something happened to abort the mission. Then Meno and his minions were left to pick up the pieces and start over," Reese offered.

"Yeah. Start over with us," I replied glumly.

"Hey, don't be so sad," Reese said as he hugged me. "We get to be cabin mates."

"I'm not so sure their motives were entirely aboveboard. What better way to keep us under surveillance than by keeping us together?"

"True, but I wonder if their monitoring equipment is nonexistent on the Red Planet or perhaps it's nonfunctioning. There's definitely a reason they put us together. We just need to use it to our advantage, not theirs."

"I hope you're right, Reese. I do hope you're right." When I put my shoe back on, Reese and I both looked at the hole I had dug with my toe. It was long and deep, like a canyon, like a Grand Canyon. I kicked sand with my shoe to cover it back up before we left

•

# Chapter 35 – Simon2

As Debarkation Day approached, we Earthlings—as we now knew the crew called us among themselves—prepared to leave the ship. We bundled up our possessions and some took clippings of plants or seedlings from the greenery on Maxwell Street.

I pulled out all my old clothes and undergarments from the wall cabinet and laid them out on the bed. As I began to fold them, I felt a lump in one of my bras. There was Simon's intelligence chip hidden inside. I had completely forgotten about it.

"Replicator. I need a replacement for Simon. An exact replacement."

"Not authorized. Unable to process your request," was the response.

"Who can authorize my request?"

There was a long silence. Then finally the replicator responded, "Captain Meno, Ginny, Tommy …". I stopped listening at the name of my ex.

"Tommy?" I asked the replicator, just to be sure I had heard correctly.

"Yes, Thomas-Tommy-TAO, The Ancient One."

Perfect, I thought to myself. I am going to ask for a robot to replace the one I lost when Tommy moved out.

Catching sight of Tommy in The Strike Pocket made my heart hurt. He looked great. His blue eyes hidden behind pink-tinted glasses twinkled. His beard was scruffy brown and curly. It had grown and was now a few inches below his chin. His mustache had grown too to cover his top lip. Tommy wore his hair long now. It covered his ears when it flopped forward. Often, his hair would be pulled back, like today.

And he wore an old beat up yellowy-beige cowboy hat. He had a great physique when I first met him: broad shoulders from years of playing softball and some girth to his thighs and legs -- not skinny stork legs like some men had.

Today he wore a blue jean jacket over a light blue T-shirt and blue jeans. I was pretty sure he was getting ready to perform. Out of the corner of my eye, I could see the other band members getting up on the stage.

"Tommy, can I speak with you for a minute?" I asked.

Tommy turned to look at me. For a brief moment, I could see something pass through his face, like he really remembered me. Then in a flash, it was gone, as if some other programming had taken over. I wondered if he too was infected with those nanosites? "Tommy, I need a favor. I would like another robot to replace Simon."

"Can't you just ask the replicator to make you one?"

"Well, yes, but I am not authorized to ask for one to be built."

"And?" Tommy took a swig of his beer and paused, waiting for my answer.

"Well, there are several people who can authorize me to get one. And one of those people is you."

"Really? Okay. When I get off work, I'll take care of it."

"That would be great. I'd really like to have Simon before we leave the ship. I could use his help with some things." I tried to give a sense of urgency to the issue without alarming Tommy. I was afraid if I left the ship without Simon's replacement, I might never get him.

"Got it. Sorry. Gotta go." Tommy took another swig, which emptied his beer. The beer made a hollow sound as Tommy set the bottle down on the counter. As swiftly as he did that, a waitress scooped it up and placed it on her brown metal serving tray to be disposed of. I secretly hoped the replicator would be as swift at getting me my robot.

Tommy was as good as his word. Simon2 arrived the day we were to leave the ship.

"Nice to see you again, Miss Margaret." Simon2 greeted me.

"Are you an exact replica of the Simon that Thomas and I had on Earth?" I asked.

"Yes, with a few enhancements of course." Simon2 responded. "I now have GPS set for the Red Planet, 1,013 more song sheets with lyrics, and an expanded library."

"An expanded library, you say? How is it organized?"

"Well, there are folders for different types of books, like mysteries, historical, westerns, and one for Tommy."

"What's in the Tommy folder?" I asked.

"Not authorized. I am sorry Miss Margaret, but Tommy would need to give you permission to access his private library."

"Ok. I'll ask. Can you tell me when Tommy's folder was created?"

"About a fortnight ago."

I mentally counted back to the night of my out-of-body experience, when I heard Captain Meno tell Ginny to give Tommy the mission information, whatever that was. This folder was created after that night. Somehow, Reese and I needed to gain access to that reading material.

# Chapter 36 – The Arrival

Reese had warned me not to be shocked when we landed. He was right, of course. The cloaking mechanism on the spacecraft didn't exist in our new environs. Our fellow travelers had all reversed aged. Some were in their late 20s, like Tommy. Others like Ruth and Herman were in their 40s. It was unclear why the variation, but genetics probably played a roll.

Reese and I were in our late 30s. The irony was I was nearer in age to my granddaughter than my own daughter.

Reese and I headed to our new quarters, with Simon2 in tow. Ginny had her artificial smile on as she directed us and others to our quarters, but underneath I knew she was seething when she saw Simon2 and learned that Tommy had authorized him.

"Did we really need a robot?" Reese had asked me on the holodeck before we left the ship.

"Yes. When we were packing up our stuff, I found a copy of the intelligence chip from our Earth Simon. Aidan had told me how to 3D print one before we were kidnapped. I figured we could swap it out and use him to help us get off this planet."

Reese just smiled and shook his head. "I should have known you were up to something. You and your great grandson just may have careers on the ZTeam after all."

In our quarters, Reese took out a device from his black duffel bag and palmed it. Then he walked around the room, opening storage bins. Moving chairs around, all on the pretense of making our new quarters home. In reality, he was scanning for devices. He didn't find any, but didn't seem comfortable talking in front of Simon2. I guess I had been around Reese long enough that I could read his thoughts. When he didn't say anything before slipping the device back into the duffel bag, I didn't ask.

"Simon2, do you need to power down?"

"Very good, Miss Margaret. One of my sensors is offline and I need to run a diagnostic. If you don't need me, I'll be in repair mode." Simon2 rolled himself over to a corner and seemingly shut down, although various lights blinked from time-to-time.

"The room is clear. Not sure Simon2 is though," said Reese. The uniforms we once wore no longer transformed, so they were just that--uniforms--and baggy ones, but even so, Reese looked ruggedly handsome. "However, once we swap out the chips, he should be."

Reese had caught me daydreaming. "You were a planet away there for a minute. I said the room is good but I'm not so sure about Simon2. When do you want to swap chips?" He repeated with a smile.

"Not just yet. We probably need to find out what's in Tommy's library first."

"I don't see a replicator in our room so we'll have to be very stingy with our shimmer powder," Reese said. "And just to be safe, let's not talk about anything relevant to our plans in front of Simon2 until we've swapped out the chips."

I nodded in agreement and looked at the two beds. As if reading my thoughts, Reese answered, "I'll take the one by the entrance." We'd been doing that a lot lately—able to answer each other without a word. When that started, I really couldn't say. It was probably after Thomas, rather Tommy, The Ancient One, served me with the six-word divorce document. Even though that was just a few months ago, it seemed like a lifetime. And maybe in a sense it was, for much had happened during our journey, and we still needed to figure out how to get home. Home, that is what sustained me. I was pretty sure that is what sustained Reese too. He needed to complete his mission. And maybe that was my mission too. And Aidan's.

We unpacked the few belongings we brought with. Reese still had the communications device. He looked around the room for a suitable hiding space. I pressed a button on Simon2. A small storage slot opened up. The communications device just fit inside.

When I tried to put the intelligence chip in there too, Reese shook his head and indicated I should keep it on me. I turned my back and tucked it into my bra. Now, why I turned my back was a surprise to even me. I guess my Catholic upbringing still was in my veins. I was a bit flushed when I turned back around, embarrassed by my modesty, but Reese either didn't notice or, if he had, chose to ignore it.

There was a knock on our door. "Mess Hall," was the response when Reese said, "Yes?"

We both looked around the sterile room once more and, satisfied with the results, we headed to the Mess Hall, wherever that was, by following the others.

Captain Meno in whites greeted us in what looked to be an oversized cafeteria. Silver metal tables and chairs were spread throughout. The captain motioned for us to sit near him. Funny, it seemed like church. Everybody wanted to sit on the aisle and near the back. When we were all seated, he said, "Greetings Red Planet Inhabitants." Someone jeered, "Hey, we're Martians now."

A bit confused, Captain Meno consulted with Ginny, who was standing behind him wearing sterile white also, whispered to him. "Ah, I see," Captain Meno replied. "Greetings Martians!" There was a round of war whoops.

"I trust you've all settled into your quarters. As you may have noticed, there are no replicators in the rooms. They can be found in common areas. Additionally, the Mess Hall will serve as our dining room, meeting space and entertainment area. There will be a holodeck as soon as it is functional and one of my capable crew can show you there. Meal times are posted on the digital boards around the BioSphere.

I will need a few volunteers to venture outside. This is a dangerous environment for you humans, er Martians (everyone tittered). We will provide the outer garments you need for protection and one of our crew will accompany you on all outside trips to safeguard you and ensure that each and every volunteer returns safely to the base. If you wish to volunteer, see Ginny after this meeting."

When the meeting ending, Reese was already talking to Ginny while I was just standing up. How he moved so fast at times surprised me. Training, I thought.

"Did you receive Simon2," Tommy asked. I wasn't even aware he had come up next to me, so intent was I on staring at Reese and Ginny.

"Why yes, Tommy. Thank you so much. Simon2 will make it all seem much more like home," I responded. My heart still bumped a bit louder when I talked to Tommy. But I knew it wouldn't go any further. He was beyond my reach at the moment, and I didn't know if I would ever be able to put us back together.

"Good," he said. "Ginny gave me hell. Actually, it was quite funny to watch her lose her cool for a moment, but she got over it. After all, I am Tommy, The Ancient One." He winked at me as Patty tucked her arm into his and whispered into his ear. "Gotta go, M. See ya around."

Reese walked up as I was still shaking my head, smiling. "What did Tommy want?" Reese asked.

"He just wanted to make sure I had received Simon2. As we suspected Ginny was not happy at all that he authorized the robot. Funny, but he called me M, which was a nickname he used when he wanted to be playful."

"Playful, huh?" Reese said as he watched Tommy and Patty stop to see Ginny. From the distance we were at, it appeared that Tommy wanted to sign up as a volunteer. We could see Ginny shaking her head no. I wondered why Ginny wouldn't let Tommy volunteer, and I was sure Reese thought the same because I could see the questioning look in his eyes.

"Ginny wasn't too eager to put my name on the volunteer list, but then I reminded her that I was one of Tommy's assistants," he said.

"Did she say what the volunteers would be doing?" I asked as we exited the hall.

"Not at the moment. We're to meet in Quadrant 6 tomorrow at 8 am. Let's walk around a bit so I can get oriented."

Reese and I explored every hallway, every room that would open. We found the holodeck and where Maxwell Street would be reborn at end of one of the corridors. The layout of Home Base was like a giant hash mark, which actually seemed odd. Why not make the base a large square, or rectangle, or even round, I mused? I couldn't imagine why there was wasted space at the edge of the hash marks. Of course, we were going to use one area for Maxwell Street. Maybe all the end areas eventually would be converted to green space or garden centers.

# Chapter 37—The Survey Crew

For Reese, the experience outside the BioSphere was breathtaking and surreal, like a Dali painting. Here he was on Mars.

"Long distance vision," Reese commanded his headset. As soon as he said the words, a vision board appeared in his helmet, allowing him to magnify the surrounding terrain. He confirmed with his onsite computer that he was in the Valles Marineris. He began looking for something very specific, but he didn't see it anywhere, thinking he'd have to check with Simon2 later.

Herman tapped on his headgear, bringing Reese back to the present. "Close," Reese commanded the vision board.

Herman tapped on his headgear again and pointed to what looked like his ear. Reese shook his head. He couldn't hear anything inside his helmet. Herman motioned for Reese to watch him. Herman pointed to some rocks on the ground. He picked one up and loaded it onto the Martian Rover Vehicle that was behind him. Herman motioned that five more rocks were needed. Reese helped load them—and then they boarded the MRV to head back to base camp.

Inside the decompression chamber, Herman asked, "Reese, why did you turn off the sound in your helmet?"

Reese responded, "I didn't."

Herman replied, "I'll have one of the crew check it out."

Reese was a bit wary. He knew he hadn't shut off anything—and using the long-range scanning device should not have done anything, so the question was why? What had happened so he couldn't hear the others? He thought maybe Simon2 could answer the question.

Returning to our shared quarters, I could tell Reese was excited. "I didn't notice any difference in gravity, although Gavin, the crew member who accompanied us, said it was due to the design of our suits. And the ground was red sand, similar to what you might find in the Southwest, like Arizona."

Simon2 responded, "Yes, the ground on the Red Planet is similar to that of Western United States."

"It seemed like we walked for a long time, but the terrain rarely changed. The mountains still seemed as far off as they were when we started walking."

"It was an optical illusion caused by the sun reflecting off the sandy soil, similar to a mirage, where you think you see water in the distance." Simon2 offered.

"Simon2, I had a problem today. I couldn't hear the others in my headset." Reese said.

Simon2 was quick with a response. "Fellow travelers are able to hear one another using nanotechnology."

There was that word *nanotechnology*. Reese and I surely didn't want Ginny and her crew to find out we weren't infected by the nanosites. This was definitely going to be a problem.

# Chapter 38 – Hearing Devices

Ginny caught up to Reese during dinner in the Mess Hall. "You had problems with the communicator in your head gear?" She eyed him carefully."

'Yes. Herman asked me if I had turned off the device. I didn't think I had, but I must have. Sorry. Rookie mistake," Reese said looking appropriately apologetic.

Ginny just nodded and walked away.

"Why do I have the feeling Ginny thinks I'm lying?" Reese asked me later in the privacy of our quarters.

Simon2 responds, "Because you are."

Reese sucked in his breath. "Simon2, you can't say such stuff."

"But I just did," replied Simon2.

"But you can't—or shouldn't."

"But it's correct."

"Simon2, on this planet, being correct can kill you."

Simon2 responded, "Clarification. You mean *you* not *me*."

"Correct. Simon2, add filter to block saying whether an individual is lying or not."

After a few lights flickered on and off, Simon2 responded, "Done."

"Simon2, I was looking for the Einstein electric automobile sent to the Red Planet. Our survey crew didn't locate it today. It would have been fun to find it and see if it will start."

"Einstein, an electric vehicle with lithium ion battery energy storage and solar roof panels," Simon2 announced with the diction of a teacher, enunciating each word slowly so all could grasp its meaning. It landed in the Valles Marineris in 2020." Simon2 then quoted verbatim from the *Tribune Standard* article outlining the accomplishment. There were even pictures from an orbiting satellite showing its location, which Simon2 projected on the wall.

"Was there an update to that information?" Reese asked Simon2.

"Negative," Simon2 responded.  "I'd like to power down now, Miss Margaret."

I replied, "Ok."

Reese was pretty sure he had been looking in the right direction earlier today to be able to see where the Edison had landed—and yet there was nothing.
As soon as Simon2 shut down, Reese and I began discussing his inability to hear the survey team members.  "Why not have Simon2 make a device so you can hear what they hear? Actually, we'll need two in case they start using them in the BioSphere. We definitely don't want them to find out we're not infected. That would be disastrous for us," I said.

Reese said, "Not to say deadly. I'm pretty sure they wouldn't hesitate to extinguish us—isn't that the word they used before?"

"Yes," I said. My brow had a deep worry furrow. I was feeling our window to escape was closing. I was very worried indeed. Reese and I talked and talked. When we'd figured out a plan, I had Simon2 power up and asked for earbuds so we both could enhance what others heard.

Simon2 said, "I will need some supplies." Simon2 ticked off a list, and Reese was able to locate most of them within our quarters.

"A filament," Reese said aloud. We didn't have that, but he had an idea where to get one.

The next morning, Reese and I headed to the new Maxwell Street area. It was still being developed. The only things in place were a few trees and handmade signs. Reese busied himself with looking at the position of all the trees, finally deciding on one he could move that was in close proximity to a light fixture. He nodded at me.

On cue, I said, "Oh Reese, that tree isn't near enough to the light to survive. It would be a shame to lose it after our journey. Do you think you can shift the tree a tad to the left?"

Reese made a big show of shifting the tree, first positioning it in one spot, then moving it a bit, until finally he was able to shift it so much, the top of it hit the light receptacle shattering the glass.

Immediately, Gavin, one of the crew hurried down the corridor and said, "Destroying property, Reese?".

"No sir. I'm a bit embarrassed. I was sure I could handle shifting the tree by myself but I miscalculated the height. Let me clean up." Reese reached down and started picking up the broken glass and filaments.

Gavin stopped him, "We have a team to clean up and replace the fixture." Reese set down the pieces of glass he had already gathered and deftly dropped the filaments into his pocket.

Gavin looked at Reese's hands. Reese held them up, showing there was nothing in them. "We wouldn't want you to be cut on the glass," he said.

Reese again offered his apologies, "I am so sorry for my faux pas."

Gavin replied, "Faux pas? Faux pas? Ah, French for a mistake. Yes, of course. Understandable. After all, you are human. Is the flower where you wanted it?"

"Yes, yes, it is. It will get good light now to grow," Reese responded, not even correcting Gavin that it was a tree, not a flower.

Reese and I left the area. We wanted to go back to our quarters, but decided against it. Just before we walked into the Mess Hall, Reese handed the filaments to me. I slipped them into my bra. Good thing, too. Ginny was waiting to greet us.

"Hello Reese and Margaret. I heard about your little mishap in Maxwell Street," Ginny said.

Ever the English language scholar, corrosively I said, "*On*, it's *on* Maxwell Street, not *in*."

Reese flinched, but did not question why I was choosing this time to be so precise.

"I stand corrected—*on* Maxwell Street." The scanner Ginny held in her hand went off. "What are you hiding, Margaret? My scanner detects metal."

"Of course, there's metal. It's in my bra. It's called a stay," I responded, unruffled.

Ginny says aloud, "Stay, stay. Don't move. Stay, stay. Whale bone in women's undergarment to offer support. Archaic. Stay, stay. Metal or plastic to offer proper support." Ginny slowly nodded her head. "Have your Simon2 replace the metal with some other type of support." Ginny turned on her heels and walked away. Her shoes had a faint clicking sound.

When I finally looked at Reese, for during the whole exchange I dared not, I saw the smallest bead of sweat on his brow. We headed to the bar without talking and ordered beers.

Back in our quarters, I reached into my bra and pulled out the filaments for Simon2. The robot worked quickly to replicate nonmetallic filaments to work in the ear buds—and then presented them to Reese and me to test. Just in time too. Reese was scheduled to be on the survey team again the next morning.

We wore our new devices to the Mess Hall that evening. We could hear everything. It almost seemed like we could read people's thoughts, although that wasn't entirely true. It just felt like it with the huge amount of noise we could now hear. Others seemed oblivious to the din, so we acted likewise. It was only when Captain Meno walked to the front of the room and cleared his throat that everyone got quiet.

"Thank you for enduring the space travel so well and the transition to our Mars BioSphere. Teams are surveying our present coordinates and working on a plan for a long-term water supply, a requirement to sustain human life. The inside crews have been busy re-establishing some of the life centers you previously found enjoyable or frequented. While the holodeck is not yet functioning, Maxwell Street is being revitalized here on Mars." Captain Meno had a few more platitudes for the group before closing with a toast, "To Mars, your new home!"

All raised their beverages, alcoholic or otherwise, and toasted with Captain Meno, including Reese and I as Ginny watched us from the sidelines. She leaned over and said something to one of her crew, who looked straight at us.

# Chapter 39 – The Work Crews

The next morning I worked on a Maxwell Street detail. Simon2 had scanned me, so I knew no metal would be detected, and it was a good thing. Ginny showed up and stood near me, holding her scanning device.

"Well—you must have replaced your metallic stays with another material. Your scans are clear," Ginny said.

"Yes. I did address the situation as soon as you pointed it out." I practically cooed in response, anxious for the encounter to be over.

"Very good," Ginny responded and walked off, her soft shoes clicking off into the distance.

I was worried. It was becoming more dangerous to be here. We have to have a plan, I thought. When I was released from my work detail, I made my way back to our quarters.

When Reese entered the room, I asked, "Well? How did everything go?"

"Much better. I could hear everybody. No sign yet of the electric car."

"I have something we may want to try," I said as I reached my hands around under my shirt to the back of my bra.

Reese replied, "You're sure we're ready for this?"

I blushed and said, "Just wait." In a few seconds, I pulled out an intelligence chip. "It's Simon's—the Simon we had back on Earth. Remember I told you about the chip when we first arrived."

"Your wonders never fail," Reese said.

I walked over to Simon2 and told him, "Sleep mode." Immediately all the lights shut off. Removing Simon2's intelligence chip, I inserted the old one from Earth. For a few minutes, there was nothing. No lights. No noise. Nothing. Reese gave me a questioning glance.

Then Simon2 woke up and greeted me. "Margaret. How good to see you again. It seems like I have been recharging a long time." Simon2 looked around the room. "And you are not Thomas. You are Reese."

"Simon, Reese is helping me," I said. Not giving Simon a chance to ask any more questions about Thomas, I continued, "Where are we?"

"We are in the Barring Crater in southwestern Arizona."

"What?" Reese and I both said.

"Jinx on you," Simon said. He double checked their location and repeated his response.

I had almost forgotten Simon2 had a human chip embedded in him. "You're not being funny, are you Simon?" I asked. "We're supposed to be on Mars."

"Perhaps my GPS is off. I can run a diagnostic if you like," Simon2 responded.

Reese shook his head. "No, that's okay for the moment," Margaret responded.

"Simon, can you tell me if an electric car landed in the Marinas Trench in 2020?"

"Yes," and Simon quoted from various news articles he had stored, including one from the *Tribune Standard*.

Reese nodded his head and said, "I thought so."

"Shall I swap the chips back?" I asked.

"Yes. We don't want Ginny noticing the other Simon2 is offline."
As I swapped chips, I asked Reese what he thought of the information.

Reese's first reaction was that Simon2's GPS was not working properly because he was off during their space flight. But he did have an idea on what to do about the *Tribune Standard* info.
"Wake Simon2, Margaret."

Simon2 came alive and asked, "Margaret, is there something I can help you with?"

"Can you help me pick up the place?" I said.

Simon2 responded, "Not possible. Too heavy to pick up."

"Can you help me straighten our quarters?" I revised.

Simon said, "Straighten, to uncurl, or to level, or to tidy. You want me to tidy the quarters?"

"Yes,' I responded.

Behind Simon2's back, Reese nodded at me, and said, "Margaret, did you know . . . ." repeating what the Earth Simon had told them about the electric car. He also included some information the Earth Simon had not said, but I knew better than to stop him. I knew the information was not really for me.

# Chapter 40 – The Vista

Reese didn't go out on survey detail for a few days. When he did go again, he waited for an opportunity to scan the vista for the red electric car. Sure enough, there it was. Just as he thought it should be and just as he told Simon2 where it would be.

Herman asked him, "What are you looking at?"

Reese responded, "Just the view. It's amazing I'm standing here on Mars. No one back on Earth would believe me."

Herman said, "There's no one back on Earth to tell. They're all gone— remember? Our home was destroyed."

"Yes, I know. What I meant was if there were anyone to tell, they wouldn't believe me."

"Right," said Herman, but he had a strange look on his face.

We have to get out of here before we can't, Reese thought, somewhat mad at himself for his slip-up.

That night back in our quarters, Reese made sure to tell me about all the equipment stored in the electric car, which still should be drivable. He repeated that information several times in front of Simon2 just to make sure he heard it all-every detail, every word. Reese knew he had to get me to join him on his next survey detail.

Reese told Simon2, "Ginny asked me to bring you tomorrow on our next expedition. And it's not a mirage. The red electric car is a lot closer than it looks. We will be allowed to explore it tomorrow."

I said nothing and let Reese ramble on about what was going to happen and when. I knew the showdown was coming, even without the communications device in my ear. I could sense it.

The next day Reese and I headed to the airlock to suit up. We hurriedly dressed and exited the BioSphere before anyone saw us. Once outside, Reese commanded his visor to show him where the electric car was. As he had stated, it was much closer and easily reachable. Reese and I started toward the car.

It wasn't long before Ginny exited the BioSphere and saw Reese and someone else heading toward the car.

"Reese, where are you going?" Ginny asked in his headset. "And who is that with you?"

Reese acted like he couldn't hear. He turned around and pointed to his helmet—and shook his head no. And then he pointed to the car and held out his scanner indicating he wanted to scan the car.

Ginny screamed in his headset. "No, no. You're too far away from the BioSphere."

But Reese and I continued anyway. I was very careful not to look back so she wouldn't know I was with him.

Ginny shouted again at Reese, "Who is that with you?

Gavin said something to Ginny, but Reese wasn't able to catch all the words.

Ginny shouted again, "Reese, stop! Is that Margaret with you? She's not in her quarters."

But Reese ignored her questions. It wouldn't do to respond, then Ginny would know he could really hear her.

Ginny commanded Gavin, "Take one of the crew with you on the MRV and bring them back."

Reese and I picked up our pace. As we approached the car, Reese indicated that I should remove my helmet. I looked at him and shook my head no. He opened the car door to show two portable oxygen containers inside. I nodded my head in agreement. I opened the car door and sat down. My helmet clunked against the side of the car. I pulled it off as Reese instructed and put on the portable oxygen mask, holding my breath all the while until connected again.

Reese heard Ginny in his headset lamenting, "Margaret. I knew I should have extinguished you when I had the chance."

Reese removed his helmet so both of us were sitting in the car with the portable oxygen containers.

I tilted my head slightly, as if to indicate, "Now what?"

Reese tapped the power button and the Edison started up. He put the car into gear and hit the accelerator, just in time. Gavin and Rodney just rounded the mound, close on our tail.

The Edison had one advantage. It was built for speed and speed it did have. Reese was able to quickly put distance between us and the MRV. Reese indicated for me to listen to the headset to find out what was going on.

Gavin reported to Ginny, "They have a sizable lead. Do you want us to pursue?"

Ginny replied, "No. Let me formulate a new plan. Return to base camp."

For the first time, Reese exhaled after I signaled that our pursuers were returning to base camp.

# Chapter 41 – Now What?

I should have been elated that we had escaped our captors, but truthfully I was scared. I hoped leaving the shelter of the BioSphere wouldn't be our death sentence.

Reese said nothing but kept driving. Occasionally he'd check our coordinates against a GPS device he had smuggled onto the starship when we were first abducted.

Eventually he stopped the car, again checking the GPS coordinates before shutting off the engine. What lay in front of us was a sheer rock wall.

Reese asked, "How are your rock-climbing skills?

I responded, "Are you serious?" The red wall seemed to go up for miles.

Reese said, "Yes, I'm deadly serious. We need to get up that rock face today. Tomorrow might be too late. But we will have some help. You'll need to put your helmet back on. We're exiting the vehicle. This as far as we can go in the Edison."

We both exited the car with our helmets on. Reese opened the trunk and pulled out some gear. One was a strange pulley device attached to an arrow cannon.

Reese commanded his headset to magnify the rock wall. He continued to scan the rock face until he found what he was looking for. Making note of the exact GPS location, he entered the coordinates into the ultrasonic arrow cannon. "Margaret, step clear of the rope." When I was a safe distance away, he fired. The arrow drove into the rock ledge, taking nearly the full length of double rope with it.

Reese tugged on the line several times. Satisfied it would hold, he indicated for me to step into the harness and then clipped my restraint to one of the loops on the rope. He grabbed the duffel bag still in the trunk and clipped it to another loop. Then he put on a backpack and stepped into the last harness and clipped himself to a loop.

Reese put the pulley contraption in the car and turned on the portable oxygen packs. Leaving the door slightly ajar, Reese leaned over to start the engine on the pulley. It reminded me of an old lawn mower or a motorboat- -engines with pull starts.

Once the pulley engine started, the slack in the rope was rapidly taken up— and I was jerked skyward, toward the rock wall. Our gear was next and then Reese followed. If we had had enough time, Reese would have spaced us out. He hoped his calculations were correct. Otherwise they could run out of fuel or oxygen halfway up or have the rope slip or fray. It wasn't anything he was interested in finding out about.

As they were propelled skyward, Reese noticed Mars dust rising near the Edison.

"Ginny and her goons," he thought. Margaret and he were almost to the top when the pulley stopped.

With just seconds to spare, Reese started the jet pack on his back, hoping to be able to bounce to freedom. He unhooked his crampon and the duffel bag, which he flung onto the rock top. I was now being jerked backward on the pulley system. By the look on my face, Reese knew I was terrified. Reese unhooked me and together we landed on the top.

We lay there for several long minutes, just trying to gauge how close we came.

Gavin found the ultrasonic arrow cannon near the Edison. It took him a few minutes to figure out how the device worked, but once he did, he aimed it precisely at where we were.

"Roll," Reese commanded, pushing me to one side as he rolled the opposite way. The arrow breezed past the two of us, close enough to cause a tear in Reese's suit. He fumbled in the duffel bag, pulling out what looked like duct tape. Ripping off a piece, he put it on the rip.

Motioning to me, we crawled away from the rock face. Reese snuck a peek with his scanner to see Gavin loading the ultrasonic arrow cannon again.

Reese pointed to the back wall of the rock ledge. I crawled there, as did Reese. The next arrow has an explosive device attached that caused part of the rock ledge to shatter, sending shrapnel into the air.

Reese pulled me to my feet and we started running, away from the cliff edge. We ran at an angle to stay hidden from below. Reese knew there were at least three more arrows left. He'd wanted to make sure they would have had enough equipment to escape. Unfortunately, their escape equipment might well seal their fate if they couldn't put enough distance between them and the rock ledge.

Two more arrows whizzed past them into the rock ledge, again sending shards in all directions.

One more arrow left. Reese pulled me behind a boulder and pushed me down flat. We had run as far as we could for now and waited for the detonation. It was massive. This time boulders rolled past and dust encircled us. Reese caught a glimpse of a drone flying toward us. He kept his head down and prayed I didn't move a muscle. The drone hovered over our bodies for a long time.

In his headset, Reese heard Gavin reporting, "Mission accomplished. The boulder flattened them. They are extinguished."

Ginny responded, "Good. We will tell the others they were lost on the surveying mission."

The drone flew off and Reese breathed a sigh. He pulled out his GPS device. "Crap," he mouthed silently. The face was cracked.

Reese held a gloved finger to his lips, motioning for me to remain silent. He was pretty sure Ginny was still monitoring their transmissions.

He showed me his broken GPS device and shrugged his shoulders to indicate what next. He looked onto the horizon, trying to figure what direction was the best heading.

I thought for a bit, remembering all the time Reese and I had spent at the beach and the position of the stars on the few occasions we were there at dusk.

While Reese pointed in a northeast direction and mouthed, "North," I shook my head no. I closed my eyes and thought of my family, of my great grandson Aidan, and then opened them. I remembered. In my pocket, I carried the SpaceTime device. Besides being a communications and gaming device, it also had a compass in it. To my surprise, it worked. Mars must have magnetic poles, I thought, like Earth. I handed it to Reese.

Reese nodded and smiled. Due north. That was the direction they needed to head and quickly.

As we walked in our spacesuits, fatigue set in. We had been on the go since daybreak. I didn't know how much further I could go. I was so thirsty. Reese noticed me lagging and stopped. He motioned to an outstretch of rocks so we could sit down. While seated, he checked the air in our tanks. Not much left. He pulled me to my feet and motioned with his fingers that we had to keep walking. I nodded, but the exhausted look on my face said it all.

We walked another few miles before our air supply started to give out. First it sputtered, then it just stopped. Reese took off his helmet. I did the same. We held our breath as long as possible for our final goodbye. Tears were running down my face. Reese's steely eyes were soft and brimming. How had I seen him so differently before? I had so much to say and no breath to do it. I crumpled to the ground. Reese fell to the ground himself.

# Chapter 42 – The ZTeam

When the ZTeam located Margaret and Reese, they weren't too sure if they were still alive. They carried them to waiting ambulances where their vitals were taken.

Walter was there, grumpy as ever. He so wanted to smoke, but couldn't as oxygen cups were placed on Margaret and Reese and fluids administered. He wouldn't be getting any answers today.

It was a day later when I finally woke up in what looked like a hospital. Ginny and her crew had recaptured us, I thought. Disappointment stung in my eyes. I threw off my covers and swung my feet over the edge of the bed, ready to make a run for it. That's when I heard his voice.

"Whoa. Now hold on." Reese said. He was dressed in jeans and a white shirt. No hospital clothes for him. He had been so still I hadn't noticed him sitting in the room before.

"We have to get out of here before they extinguish us," I said in a low voice, furtively looking around the room.

Reese stood by the edge of the bed and put his arms on my shoulders. My eyes were wide, darting madly around the room, looking for ways to escape.

"Margaret, Margaret, look at me." Reese commanded. "You're safe. We're back on Earth."

It took a few seconds before I was able to comprehend what Reese was saying. "On Earth, but how? How did we get off Mars?"

"Well, that's the thing. We never were on Mars. The spaceship landed in the Barringer Crater near Winslow, Arizona. It's pretty close to Flagstaff. It's 3,900 feet in diameter and 560 feet deep. The spaceship used some type of holodeck program to alter the atmosphere to match that of Mars." Reese said. "That's probably why the holodeck didn't work inside the BioSphere. They were using it outside."

I struggled to stand up. I did my best thinking while pacing. Reese relaxed his grip on my shoulders and helped me with the slippers the hospital had provided, along with a white robe to cover my blue pajamas.

After walking back and forth several times on the gray tiled floor, I finally stopped and looked up at Reese, my hands stilled balled up in my robe pockets. "You've got to be kidding. It was all a ruse? What of the others? Were they rescued?"

Before Reese could answer, there was a knock on the door and Walter entered.

"Cliff, so good to see you again." Walter shook hands with Cliff, and then gave him an uncharacteristic hug. "And this must be Margaret, your accomplice." Walter shook hands with Margaret, clasping his second hand over hers. "The ZTeam much appreciates your assistance, much appreciates."

All I could think to say, "Reese orchestrated our escape. I just tagged along."

"Reese? Ah, Cliff, yes, he's one of our best but from what I understand you helped him greatly, especially with your SpaceTime device. I met with your great grandson Aidan. He told me all about it." Walter said.

"So, what happened to the others? Were you able to rescue them?" I asked, sitting down in one of the chairs, suddenly very weary.

Walter shook his head. "No. By the time we reached the location of the spacecraft, it had taken off. I'm afraid you two were the only ones rescued."

"How did you ever find us? We were out of oxygen." I asked.

"Well, Cliff's GPS device was still working, even though the glass was cracked. We were tracking your movements. Actually, you were within a mile of the exterior of the holodeck program. You could have walked out into Earth's atmosphere if your tanks hadn't given out. We were near your location and raced in once we saw your movement had stopped."

"I suspected we were on Earth when I didn't see the Edison on the first survey mission. That's why I spent so much time giving detailed information to Simon2 where the Edison was located and what was in it. I wanted to make sure we had the supplies necessary for our escape," Reese said as he sat down next to me and held my hand.

"Thomas is still trapped?" I said slowly, taking slow sips of the information provided.

"Margaret, I'm very sorry we weren't able to rescue your husband and the others."

It took a few more minutes before I was able to respond. "I guess in the end my Thomas was lost to me many years ago." Tears rolled down my cheeks. Reese let go of my hand and grabbed a few tissues for me.

I dabbed at my face like an artist applying paint to a canvass. "So now what? Can I go home?" I asked.

"No. At least not as Margaret. But we can talk about that later. After you've had time to recover from your experience."

I just nodded.

# Chapter 43 – Monterey Blackhawk

A week later Walter arranged a press conference in Chicago. Reese and I were there, along with many of the families who had lost abducted loved ones. Walter explained what their elite squad had learned and he introduced Cliff.

Aidan was present in the crowd along with his mother and grandmother. As the crowd dispersed, but before Aidan and the others left, Buzz and Cassidy--the two men he had met before--asked them to stop by to see Walter.

Walter motioned for me to stand a ways off. He warmly shook Aidan's hand and said to his mother and grandmother, "Your boy has a job waiting for him with the ZTeam when he finishes college."

Cliff shook Aidan's hand, saying, "A pleasure meeting you, son. Great job, Aidan. I look forward to working with you in the future."

Aidan's grandmother said to Cliff, "She looks vaguely familiar. Do I know her?" and she was pointing right at me.

Cliff responded, "No, I don't believe so."

Aidan's grandmother continued, "Why she is beautiful. She kind of reminds me of my mother, but she's much more beautiful than my mother ever was."

Aidan responded, "You're wrong, Grandma. Great Nana is that beautiful."

Aidan's grandmother said, "Is?"

Aidan responded, "I meant was."

Walter asked to keep Aidan for a few more minutes. Using the excuse of ZTeam information, Walter had Buzz and Cassidy lead the others out of the room.

Waiting for my cue, Walter nodded to let me know we had a few minutes to talk.

"Is Great Papa alive?" Aidan asked.

"Oh yes, dear. He took much longer to regress than the rest of us and he regressed to a much earlier age than me. Than us, I'm afraid. He regressed to his mid-20s, just about your age and sadly before we met. He didn't know me and fell in love with someone else." I responded.

"Is he happy?" Aidan asked.

"Why yes dear. He is very happy. He's their Ancient One, their architect. No, he's their creator. I have so much to tell you, but not here. Do you still have your SpaceTime device?

"Yes," Aidan said.

"I'll contact you."

"What do I call you?"

"Why, I am Monterey Blackhawk, of course," I said and winked.

# Chapter 44 – Epilogue

Captain Meno gathered the humans in the Mess Hall. "The climate on this planet has proven toxic to human life. Please give a moment of silence to two of members, Reese and Margaret, who lost their lives while on the Survey Team."

The passengers seemed to all suck in their breaths at the same time. Shock registered on Lillian's and Ruth's faces, as tears stung their eyes.

Captain Meno said to Herman, "Would you like to say a few words?"

Herman nodded and led the group in prayer for the two members who lost their lives.

Tommy bowed his head, but he did not join in prayer. Something did not feel right to him. He didn't know why, but he sensed Margaret was still alive. Somehow, he knew this was not something he could discuss with anyone, not even Patty. This was a secret he needed to mull over.

Captain Meno then stated, "Since the planet cannot support human life, we must relocate. The starship will take off in 60 of your minutes. Please head to your quarters to make preparations."

Coming soon *SpaceTime 2047+4.*

www.ingramcontent.com/pod-product-compliance
Lightning Source LLC
Chambersburg PA
CBHW051245170626
46809CB00004B/1501